D1521298

When
Jesus
Calls

—⁓—

M A R T H A G A Y L E

WESTBOW
P R E S S®
A DIVISION OF THOMAS NELSON
& ZONDERVAN

WestBow Press books may be ordered through booksellers or by contacting:

WestBow Press
A Division of Thomas Nelson & Zondervan
1663 Liberty Drive
Bloomington, IN 47403
www.westbowpress.com
844-714-3454

ISBN: 979-8-3850-0594-9 (sc)
ISBN: 979-8-3850-0595-6 (hc)
ISBN: 979-8-3850-0596-3 (e)

Library of Congress Control Number: 2023916250

Print information available on the last page.

WestBow Press rev. date: 10/25/2023

CONTENTS

ACKNOWLEDGMENTS

As the Lord called me to write my first book, I want to thank Him for this journey. From the first words on the page until the end, I cried, laughed, and prayed, and my heart found healing on many occasions.

This journey of my life has been one that could only be given by Jesus. He has carried me, held me up, comforted me, encouraged me, and shown me the love I needed so desperately.

I want to dedicate this book to my daddy, who passed away to be with Jesus just as I finished my manuscript. My daddy was, without a doubt, one of my most incredible supporters. He was an amazing dad and one of the most selfless people I have ever met. He never had the opportunity to read my book, but I know he is with Jesus, which gives me much peace.

Daddy, I will miss you, and until I see you again, I will keep doing what you taught me, which is to desire always to love, sometimes even when it hurts.

I would also like to give God all the glory for this book, as He gave me the words to write, and I pray that the truth of the gospel changes lives. Many have been deceived into believing they are not worthy of His love. Do not believe the lie. You are worthy in Jesus's name. He loves you deeply!

In John 11:40, Jesus says, "Did I not tell you that if you believe, you will see the glory of God?"

Always believe,
Martha Gayle

1

---✦---

MARY'S HEART

Mary sat on her favorite bench in the garden at the inn where she worked. She loved spending time there. The garden was beautiful, no matter the season. The colors were always spectacular. The smell of fall was in the air, and the thought of the leaves changing into the most magnificent colors warmed Mary's heart. As her blonde hair blew in the breeze, she saw a couple of squirrels playing in the distance. Fall and spring were her favorite seasons. She was happy fall had arrived. Autumn reminded her of everything, pumpkin. Two of Mary's favorite things to do were baking and writing, and fall was a perfect time for both, she thought.

Mary loved to write and had a passion for Jesus. She spent much time writing poetry and short stories but always felt she would write a book one day. She took life seriously and believed every day was a gift. Mary had dreamed of a perfect life but had learned that in a fallen world, perfection wasn't possible. So, when Mary had questions about her life, she sat and wrote. Not often did anyone else see her writings, but she wrote from her heart about whatever was on her mind at the time. Somehow, it helped her to clear her mind or let go of something bothering her. Jesus spoke to Mary often during her writings and comforted her many times.

As she sat enjoying a quiet moment with God, she thought about her childhood and the days of playing outside with her friends, riding to school on her bike with her sisters, laughing, going on kayak rides at the lake, and fishing on the dock with a cane pole. Her dad had bought a place at the lake when she and her sisters were young, and they had made great memories there. Mary remembered how beautiful her dad's heart had been and he greatly loved his family.

One of Mary's favorite childhood memories was of the day she and her sisters decided to go hiking. During their hike, they'd grabbed a fishing pole and a half loaf of bread to fish with. Their dad had asked where they were going. "Just going on a hike, Dad," Mary had said. He then asked what they were going to have for lunch. They confidently told him they had planned to catch fish and cook them on an open fire.

However, they had not caught any fish during their adventure and were getting hungry, so they had begun heading back. While walking, they had seen their dad. He had been riding around looking for them. Looking back, she remembered the sweetest look on his face. He had stopped to ask how their hike was going. They had been happy to see their dad. He had brought hot dogs and buns, and they'd found a campsite, lit a fire, and roasted hot dogs together.

Mary wished her dad had had more times like those with her and her sisters, as that memory never left her. The memory of him protecting her had given her much-needed security.

As her mind took her back to those days, she realized how lonely she had felt and how much she wished to be loved. Unfortunately, Mary had spent many years seeking that love in all the wrong places.

Her dad had worked long hours every day except Sunday. She knew he loved her and her sisters and had been a great provider, but he had barely been at home because of the responsibility of providing. Her mom had been sick for most of Mary's childhood. Mary felt the sadness in her mom's heart. Her mom had done all she could to be a good mom, and she'd loved her family. Mary had great memories of times with her mom. Since her passing, she'd missed her every day.

Mary did not doubt that her parents had done the best they knew in raising her and her sisters, but she had a lot of unanswered questions.

Where are the priorities of parents? she thought. *How is the family structure being divided by the desires of worldly things instead of following the gospel? If our hearts were set on the things above, regardless of material possessions, wouldn't there be more peace? Hearts filled with joy and love? Do anxiety and stress come from striving for things that will never bring peace and joy, regardless of your possessions? If we are not rooted in the gospel first, do all worldly possessions lead to an empty, unfulfilled heart? Where did the ideas come from that have changed how we should live?*

After asking herself those questions, she was reminded of Matthew 6:19–21: "Do not store up for yourselves treasures on earth, where moths and vermin destroy, and where thieves break in and steal. But store up for yourselves treasures in heaven, where moths and vermin do not destroy, and where thieves do not break in and steal. For where your treasure is, there your heart will also be."

Where is my treasure? Mary asked herself.

Life had been difficult for her dad. Understanding that he was the provider had given him much stress. The expense of raising children and the medical treatments for their mom had become his focus. Mary's dad was a humble man and had ensured his family's needs were met the only way he knew how. Mary and her sisters were grateful. She remembered their dad's tiredness on Sundays, when he would sit at his desk to pay the bills and drop his head down into his hands. That had troubled her, but she knew she couldn't help him. She'd had no idea how.

She remembered the summers at church camp and being saved at a young age. She knew the Lord. The peace and closeness of the Holy Spirit were indescribable. She'd chased those feelings her entire life, as one could never have enough. Unfortunately, she was missing a vital lesson: she would never find that love in anyone else, only in Jesus! As Revelations 2:4 says, "Yet I hold this against you: You have forsaken the love you had at first."

At age seventeen, she'd met Walter. He'd shown Mary love in a way she had never experienced. They had done everything together. They'd held hands, laughed together, and had a romance in a way she had never felt. It had felt right to her. She'd loved the attention she got from him. He'd adored her. She had felt they would be together forever. He'd talked to her many times about having sex. "Let's just do it," he'd said. The decision hadn't seemed important to Walter, but Mary had felt differently.

Mary had been afraid. She hadn't wanted to have sex. She knew it was wrong but hadn't wanted him to leave her, so she had convinced herself it was right. She'd believed he would always be there if she gave herself to him. *It's just part of a great relationship, right?* she'd thought. *We will always love each other.* So, one evening, she gave in to the temptation. Her heart was changed forever.

She had realized it wasn't right. She had begun to feel more distant from God. She didn't feel young anymore. She didn't feel free. What Mary had thought was love had turned out to be the beginning of many new emotions: doubt, discouragement, unforgiveness, guilt, mistrust, and others. After Walter graduated from high school and left home for college, they'd visited as often as possible, but their love had drifted apart. Mary had to continue to move forward with a broken heart, trying to forget the pain.

In the next couple of years, after she'd finished high school and begun working a public job, life had found a way to continue, and days had turned into weeks and weeks into months. Then Mary had met Edward. He appeared to have been popular and fun; love consumed them. Although they both had worked public jobs, they had been together as often as they could be. For Mary, it had been like a storybook romance. She'd thought he felt the same.

Mary had spent much of her life dreaming of being married and having children. She'd wanted to be the best mom and hoped she would marry the perfect husband, who would also be the ideal dad. So when Edward asked her to marry him, she'd said yes.

When Mary had told her mom and dad that she was getting married, they'd agreed and helped her plan a small wedding at their church. She planned her dream wedding on a tight budget. She had also organized a small reception. Family, friends, and church members had made most of the food, except her wedding cake. Mary knew exactly what she wanted: a three-tiered cake with a stairway to the top layer on each side and bride and groom figures on top. She'd borrowed a wedding gown from a friend and felt excited about her dream of marriage becoming a reality. Her mom and dad had decided they could afford to pay an amateur photographer, and Mary was pleased.

On the day of the wedding, Mary looked beautiful but young. She'd had no idea what the future would be, but she'd known she was living in a moment that made her feel complete. She felt pretty while looking in the mirror as she put on her borrowed dress.

The preacher had stood in the front, the groom and best man stood on the left as well as the groomsmen, and the bridesmaids stood on the right. A few excited family members and friends had been there to see the wedding. The church wasn't full, but Mary was happy. As the wedding song began to play, Mary and her dad walked down the aisle toward them. When the preacher had asked her dad who would be giving her away, Mary had seen tears in her dad's eyes as he said, "Her mom and I." He then sat down. Before they'd known it, Mary and Edward had been announced as husband and wife.

They'd rented a small white wooden house that was aged and needed a lot of work. They'd had no idea what marriage would be like, and the dream of what it should have been had become a reality quickly. Playing house and discussing the future turned into months of stress, work, and responsibilities. Nevertheless, Mary continued to believe their marriage had been perfect as she strived to be the best wife. She'd felt sure they would be together forever. After all, they had gotten married and would always work out whatever came to them.

Mary had longed to be led in a way that pleased Christ. However, they barely attended church together and had never read their Bibles together. She had found her love in Edward, and even with all the trials, she never had suspected what would come next. After a short day of work, she had gone home early, thinking about what she would make for dinner. She'd loved to cook for Edward and make his favorite meals. She'd longed to please him.

As she walked into their rented house, she found him with another woman. She was confused and did not understand. Having no idea and feeling hurt, she'd walked away with nowhere to turn.

Mary had become angry, bitter, lonely, and afraid. Finally, she'd returned to the only place she knew, back home with her parents. She'd continued to blame herself, having no real idea why. *Why would he treat me that way? What did I do wrong?* Mary had had a personal relationship with Jesus and prayed often but had forgotten how important it was not to let go of His hand, leadership, and guidance. Mary remembered thinking of Proverbs 4:23: "Above all else, guard your heart, for everything you do flows from it." Mary quickly realized she had left her first love and had not protected her heart.

Months had gone by, and Mary was unable to think of anything else. "God, how could you allow him to treat me this way?" She had become bitter and angry with God. Her heart was crushed, and she had no idea how to keep going. *This is life, isn't it? It is just the way it is*; she'd thought. She had begun pouring herself into her work and continued to hide the pain of betrayal.

Often, instead of praying for God's direction, she'd lived on her feelings and emotions and made decisions that were not always comfortable for her. Not realizing it, she'd allowed the Enemy to drag her down a pit of destruction she never saw coming. She had walked away from the one who loved her most: her Savior, Jesus Christ.

Mary had prayed that God would help her use more discernment. She had been young and naive and wanted to believe that everyone around her was honest and that the world around her was good. However, she had come to understand increasingly that she was wrong. As she'd experienced heartaches and troubles, she began having trust issues that shut her down in a way she didn't like while also beginning to understand the need for forgiveness in her heart.

2

A CALL TO FORGIVE
AND A NEW FRIEND

As Mary continued to forget the pain of her past, she spent her days building her career, and in her heart, she believed her life was good. Her job continued to support her in ways she could never have imagined. Having been a shy girl for most of her life, she began to find her identity in her work at a popular resort called the Inn.

The inn was a beautiful, charming place. It had a unique character. The road leading to the inn was magical. Trees and flowers of every color lined the driveway, and the drive to the inn gave a sense of serenity and peace. Mary was grateful to be part of its daily operations.

During her years at the inn, Mary had realized that people loved her work ethic and personality. Her shyness finally had become the past, and she thrived on the acceptance and confirmation that she was right where she belonged. After two years of working as a front desk representative, she was offered and accepted the position of sales and marketing director.

Mary loved her new position and received much joy from her responsibilities. Although it brought much stress into her life as she met constant deadlines, it provided her with a great income, and her life revolved around her work. Her job became her identity.

At eight-thirty on Tuesday morning, Mary was sitting at her desk, reviewing her schedule for the day, when she looked up at the door and saw someone standing there. She had to look twice as she was startled. It was Edward. He had a bouquet of red roses in his hand.

"Mary, I'm sorry I scared you. Do you have a minute to talk?"

She cleared her throat and said, "Yes, I have a few minutes."

He looked her in the eye with tears coming down his cheeks. "Mary, I am so sorry I hurt you. Life was so beautiful for us, and I was wrong. I have since realized how wrong I was, and I wanted to see you face-to-face to ask you to forgive me if you can." He handed her the bouquet of roses. She reluctantly received them.

Mary's heart was racing. She was doing all she could to hold back tears. Finally, she said, "We were so in love, Edward. How could you do that to me? I could never have guessed that you could do that to me."

He cried as he sat there and listened to the pain coming out of her heart. "I know, Mary. I am so sorry. It has been my loss."

Mary disagreed with him and, becoming angry, looked at him and said, "Really?"

Then she caught herself and remembered what the Lord had said to her one day: "Mary, it's not what comes at you but what comes out of you that shows who you are in me."

She told him, "Edward, you broke my heart into a million pieces, and I lost so much of myself. I trusted you!"

Edward told Mary that he had been young and immature and had no idea what he was doing. "I never once considered the consequences of my choice and how it would affect you. Since that time, my heart has also been broken. She treated me just like I treated you, and now I understand fully how you feel. I desire to walk with Jesus now, Mary, and I have asked Jesus to forgive me. I know He has forgiven me, and I pray you can too."

He turned to walk out, when Mary called him back in. "Edward, it is good to see you. You look great."

He replied, "You are as beautiful as always. However, something about you has changed a little."

"It has, Edward. I have turned back to Jesus, and He is my best friend. Edward, we never made Him the center of our life. I put all my trust in you. I guess, in a sense, I made you, my god. Without us loving God first, we could not love each other. Not in a way that pleased Him anyway.

"I need to ask you for forgiveness too. Will you forgive me, Edward? The Lord has helped me realize where I also failed. When all of this happened, I only had Him to turn to, and I never want to make this mistake again. He is continuing to change my heart. I had no idea I had gotten so far away from Him. Life is different for me now."

As he walked out, Mary tried everything she could not to break down completely. She began to pray. "Lord, Edward coming in to see me has brought memories of pain back into my heart. Please remove the pain in my heart and replace it with joy. Please help me to forgive Edward. I feel the anger again, the pain, and I only want to feel love for him. Will you help me? Your Word is clear in Ephesians 4:32; you remind us to be kind and compassionate to each other, forgiving each other just as Christ God forgave us. Lord, you know my pain, and you know my heart. I pray that you will help Edward to forgive me as well. Thank you for forgiving both of us. In Jesus's name, I pray. Amen."

Mary had an appointment at 9:15. She ran to the bathroom to check her makeup and get herself together. *Oh, wow*, she thought. *I did not see that coming!*

As she arrived back at her desk, her clients were walking in the door. They planned to have their wedding reception at the inn. Mary got up from her desk and greeted them. "Hello. I'm Mary. It is so lovely to meet you." They sat down to discuss their ideas about what they had in mind. She had her laptop open to show them ideas from past wedding receptions she had organized. She showed pictures of ice sculptures and other ideas they had an interest in.

The inn had a full-time catering service with world-class reviews. The reputation was superb. She and her clients looked over everything and made decisions about flowers, food, and beverages. They seemed thrilled with their choices. The wedding reception was scheduled for the summer, so they had some time to make any changes if necessary.

They scheduled another meeting time to review and confirm all the details. Mary thanked them for coming in and was grateful they'd chosen the inn for their wedding reception. "You will be very pleased," Mary said with confidence. She felt joyful that they were both excited and looking forward to their life together.

As a gift for coming in, Mary handed them a small gift bag with a lovely candle and a note on a piece of beautiful pastel-colored paper before they left. As she gave it to them, she said, "Please do not make the same mistakes I made. This will help immensely."

They looked at each other and then back at Mary with warm smiles. Then, as they walked out, they stopped, looked at each other puzzledly, pulled out the paper Mary had placed inside the bag, and read the handwritten note together: "Though one may be overpowered, two can defend themselves. A cord of three strands is not quickly broken" (Ecclesiastes 4:12). As they looked at each other, they smiled again. They were grateful for the personal message and continued walking to the car.

Mary prayed for them as she watched them pull out of the parking lot. "Father, please guide and protect my clients. If it is not your will for them to be married, please change their circumstances. If they get married, may they live for you and allow you to lead them. I pray that he will be the head of their house under you as he seeks your guidance and direction to love her as Christ loved the church. Father, I pray she will be his helper and encourager and love him deeply. May their choices be for you, and may you bless them and give them the strength to endure their marriage until death parts them. If my testimony in some small way will help someone else, I guess it will be worth the pain. In Jesus's name, I pray. Amen."

She sat at her desk and thought about her visit with Edward and how startled she had been to see him there. She thought she had forgiven him, and she wanted to.

God spoke to her as she sat quietly, reflecting and asking for forgiveness. "Mary, none are perfect, and you are carrying a burden you must let go of. In my Word, Matthew 6:14 says, 'For if you forgive other people when they sin against you, your heavenly Father will also forgive you.' Mary, you have not always made the right choices, have you? I am calling you now to forgive Edward. Follow me, Mary. He is one of mine now, and I have forgiven him."

"I will forgive him, Father. Please help me! Thank you for showing me how wrong I was and giving me the strength to ask him to forgive me. In Jesus's name, I pray. Amen."

Mary's calendar was empty for the rest of the day, and she felt exhausted, so she decided to take the day off. She needed a friend. She grabbed her purse and got in her car. Before she started the engine, she picked up her phone to call Karen.

Karen was a fantastic and loyal friend. She was always there for Mary, and Mary loved that about her. She was also an amazing Christian girl. She loved Jesus, and her character portrayed that in everything she did.

Karen did not answer, so Mary left a message for her: "Hey, Karen, it's Mary. Call me as soon as you can. I wanted to see if we could have lunch together today."

Mary needed someone to talk to about her morning. When Karen did not answer, Mary decided to drive home. The phone rang seconds later, and it was Karen.

"Mary, are you OK?"

"Yes, Karen. I would like to have lunch together today. Are you available?"

"I am. I was going to call you anyway. When you called earlier, I was on the phone with my sister. She has a shih-tzu that is about two years old, and she cannot keep it. I thought of you at once, Mary. His name is JJ, and he is a great dog. He is already house-trained and everything. I told her I would call you and, if you agreed, we could come by to see him this evening. Are you off work for the rest of the day?"

"Karen, a dog?"

"Yes, let's go see him. We will have lunch at the vineyard, and I will let her know we will be there around two. Is that OK?"

"OK, Karen. But I do not know about the responsibility of a dog right now."

"I will see you at the vineyard in about fifteen minutes."

"Oh, and Karen, I have an appointment to see a cottage by the sea that is for sale at six tonight. Would you like to go with me?"

"Of course I would, Mary."

Mary arrived at the vineyard first, and Karen arrived about five minutes later. They quickly hugged. Mary needed that hug from her friend. Karen had no idea what kind of morning she'd had. The visit from Edward had been emotional for her. They sat down to order their lunch, and Karen asked Mary, "Are you OK?"

"Oh, Karen. Guess who came to the inn this morning."

Karen looked at her with concern. "Who, Mary?"

Mary told her about her visit with Edward.

Karen was happy he'd stopped by. She said, "Mary, that is great! I know it does not feel good now, bringing all the memories back, but sometimes God brings us back to these sad times to heal our hearts. So many times, we suppress these feelings, and they never go away. I promise our Father will help you through this, and you will feel much better." Karen asked Mary if she could pray with her.

"Of course you can, Karen!"

Karen began to pray. "Father, thank you for always knowing what is best for us. Thank you for my friend, Mary. I can't imagine my life without her. Father, I pray for her right now that you bless her by healing her heart from any pain from her marriage to Edward. Father, thank you for the courage you gave Edward to come into Mary's office to ask for forgiveness. We know that only you can restore hearts, and I pray that today, Mary finds a spirit of complete forgiveness and love for Edward, as he says he is now seeking to follow you. We pray that you reach into all our hearts and show us where you are not pleased, so most importantly, we are pure and clean before you, Father. In Jesus's name, we pray. Amen."

The conversation, as always, was positive and enjoyable. The food was terrific, and they were ready to go see JJ. Karen hoped Mary would take him, as she knew the companionship would be good for her.

Mary's heart was happy when they arrived at Karen's sister's house. Her thoughts about the responsibility of a new dog were overwhelming, but she knew she could love JJ. They pulled into the driveway, and Mary looked at Karen. She looked like a kid who was about to visit a toy store. She told Karen she hoped JJ loved her instantly; if he did, she would never be able to leave without him. They both giggled.

Karen's sister met them at the door and invited them in. Karen introduced Mary, and before she could get her name out, JJ came running into the living room. Mary bent down to say hello, and JJ wagged his tail and jumped around, seemingly excited.

"Uh-oh," said Karen. "This seems to be going very well."

Mary giggled with a childlike laugh. She found a chair and sat down. JJ never left her side. He jumped into her lap and finally settled down as Mary began to pet him. Mary said, "OK, I'll take him!" They all laughed, as they seemed to have known exactly how it would turn out. Mary's spirit was peaceful, and JJ knew it.

JJ had found a new home. They visited for a while and realized it was almost five. Mary had to be at the cottage to view it at six. Mary couldn't thank Karen's sister enough for JJ and invited her to visit anytime. They gathered his things, exchanged hugs, and then said goodbye. JJ left in her arms.

Mary set JJ on a blanket in the backseat and gave him a snack. Seeing how well he rode in the car was wonderful, and he had no problem going with Mary. It was a match made in heaven!

As they got closer to the cottage, Mary's heart sank. She began to think about moving and how her dream had always been to live in a cottage by the sea. She began to pray. *Father, you are overwhelming me today! My morning visit from Edward at my office, the knowledge that he has now received you, the reconciliation you gave by his asking me for forgiveness, and my asking him for forgiveness. My heart is being healed, and you have given me such a special gift in JJ. Thank you!*

They arrived at the cottage, and it was perfect. The yellow paint and white trim were precisely as she had hoped. The ocean was close, with a private walkway, and her heart began to race. She whispered a quick prayer. "Father, seriously?"

The Realtor had already arrived and was waiting for them. Mary held JJ as they walked up the cobblestone walkway.

Karen couldn't quit looking at the expressions coming from Mary. She was happy for her friend. The Realtor introduced herself, and they walked up the three steps onto the front deck, which overlooked the ocean. The deck had four Adirondack chairs and a small table, all painted navy blue. To the left of the large deck was a nice gas grill, which was covered to keep it out of the weather.

As they walked through the front door, Mary held JJ, and Karen was behind them. Mary couldn't speak. She looked at Karen with the biggest grin Karen had ever seen from Mary. Then she said with a tear dropping from her eye, "This may be where I finish my first book and maybe start the second one!"

The living room was charming, with beams in the ceiling and shiplap on the walls. The kitchen opened into the living room, supplying open space for entertaining. It had large windows and stainless-steel appliances with white-and-gray granite countertops. The cottage had two nice-sized bedrooms. One was on the front side of the cottage, facing the ocean, and the other was on the back side of the cottage. Both had private baths. Mary thought how nice the place would be for guests to visit. The bathrooms both had sunken tubs with jets and walk-in tile showers. With excitement, Mary said, "The place is perfect!"

They decided to walk down to the beach, and as they left, Mary stopped to take a second look at the front door. She loved it. It was a navy-blue painted Victorian-style door, and the style perfectly matched the cottage.

As they began walking down the walkway, JJ wanted to get down. She realized JJ would enjoy the beach, and he seemed excited. That made Mary happy, too.

As they were walking, Mary noticed a few boards that needed to be replaced and mentioned it to the Realtor. As they got midway along the walkway, she saw a place with a mat, a shower, and a water spigot. "Wow," she said. "This will be nice to shower off or rinse off your feet, so you're not tracking the sand to the house." They all agreed. They left their shoes there and walked the rest of the way barefoot. The temperature was chilly, but they were happy anyway.

There were only five steps down to the sand, and despite the coolness of the sand, it felt great between their toes. Mary watched the water come up onto the shore with no words. She was silent except for a quick prayer: "Father, could this be mine? Lord, please!"

The Realtor walked over to Mary and asked her what she thought. Mary surprised herself when she looked at her and said, "I'll take it!" The Realtor was not surprised.

They left the shore and walked back to the house. They stopped to wash their feet along the way.

Mary wanted to return inside again, so they all went in together. As they walked inside, she envisioned where she would place her furniture. She noticed the corner to the left in the living room. It was positioned next to a large picture window, and a gas fireplace was on the back wall. From the window, she could look out over the water. Mary realized that was the place for her favorite chair. She had thoughts of writing there.

Mary had never written a book before and was getting close to finishing her first one. She was hopeful the cottage would be where she finished it.

Before now, she had journaled a lot and written quite a bit of poetry and short stories over the years. She pictured the cottage rooms in her head and thought of pieces she had seen while shopping that would be perfect in her new cottage.

She spoke with the Realtor about deposits and such and agreed that she would make a trip to her local bank for the loan within the next couple of days. She then pulled out her wallet from her purse and wrote a check for the deposit to hold it. After that, Mary prayed that the cottage would be her and JJ's new home.

Actual photo of JJ

3

A DREAM BECOMES REALITY WHILE HEARTS ARE CHANGED

When Mary arrived at the inn, she grabbed a cup of coffee and walked into her office. After checking her schedule for the day, she realized she had a 10:00 a.m. appointment with Mr. Henry, the inn's general manager. He was a fantastic person. They had worked together for years, and they worked well together. He wanted to go over her work performance and discuss upcoming events on the schedule. Mary had a couple of hours before the meeting, so she spent time preparing. She knew she also had an appointment at lunch with the bank about her loan.

Mr. Henry was a short man and always wore expensive suits. He had a smile that lit up any room. Mary had not met anyone who didn't love him. The inn had been his life since his wife passed away five years ago. Although he often felt lonely, his job fulfilled him, and all the employees loved him. Mr. Henry always thought of them first because, being a great leader, he realized he would never have been successful without great employees. Mr.

Henry was a great listener, and his employees knew they could come to him for advice. He wasn't only their boss; he had become their friend.

The inn had set records for long-term employees, and a couple had retired there. Employee turnover was rare because of the kindness in Mr. Henry's heart.

Mary looked down at her phone and realized her meeting with Mr. Henry was in five minutes. She closed her email, grabbed her folder, and headed to his office. He was standing in front of his desk with a strange look.

"Hi, Mr. Henry. How are you?"

"Hi, Mary. I'm good." They walked into his office together. "Have a seat," he said.

The tension in the room was a little weird, Mary thought. She whispered to herself, "We have had these weekly meetings for more than five years. This feels strange." Mr. Henry was always happy, but this time, he wasn't.

Mary sat down and gave him an unusual look. He told Mary he was sick and did not think he could continue working. "I have been over your review thoroughly, and you are ready for my position."

As he did not elaborate on his condition, Mary was confused.

"You have done an outstanding job here, Mary, and everyone loves you. I can't leave here until I know the person taking my position will continue to run the inn as we have together all these years."

Mary finally got a chance to speak. "Mr. Henry, I am so sorry. What's going on?"

"Mary, I have stage-three cancer, and they are not expecting me to live very long."

Mary began sobbing. "Mr. Henry, that can't be true."

"I know, Mary. It is true, and I am very sad, but I know God will get me through this. Thank you, Mary, for all our conversations about God. I have never told you this, but because of you and your witness, I have asked Jesus to come into my heart. I have chosen to follow Jesus. I realize that over the years, it appeared I wasn't interested, but I promise you I was listening."

Mary couldn't control her emotions. Her heart was broken and happy at the same time. She was sad that he was sick, but she was overjoyed that he had come to know Jesus in a personal way. She loved Mr. Henry. He had been good to her over the years, and she couldn't imagine her life without him. She got up from her chair and walked over to him. "Can I hug you?"

"Of course, you can." They hugged, and he comforted her. "It's going to be OK. I will not leave this world until the good Lord wants me to, and there are lots of people praying for healing for me. Now, tell me you will take this position."

She told Mr. Henry she would think about it but knew the answer would be no. She hugged him again and said, "You have another praying friend here—don't forget. I will be praying for you and am so proud of you for choosing Jesus! You have made the best decision you will ever make."

He smiled at Mary and said, "I know, Mary. I know."

She excused herself and told him she knew he needed an answer quickly, and she would tell him tomorrow.

Mary had an appointment in forty-five minutes at the bank, and she needed to run home quickly. During the drive home, Mary prayed for Mr. Henry. "Father, my heart is so sad. He has been so good to me for so many years now. His doctor says he has cancer. Father, I know you are the Great Physician. Father, in Isaiah 53:5, in your Word, you say, 'But He was pierced for our transgressions, he was crushed for our iniquities; the punishment that brought us peace was on him, and by his wounds, we are healed.' Father, please heal my friend and make his body whole again. In Jesus's name, I pray. Amen."

Mary's head was spinning. She was sad about Mr. Henry, and she knew she had no interest in taking the general manager's position but would tell him tomorrow. She had a book to finish and enjoyed her time at home with JJ. Although her apartment was small, it was still home. Then Mary thought, *Well, until we move into the cottage. I guess that's if we get the loan.* She began to pray. "Lord, your will be done. Amen."

Mary arrived at her apartment and went inside. JJ was happy to see her. She picked him up and ran him out to go potty, and as she brought him back inside, she said, "I will be back later, buddy; we need to do some writing today."

While driving to the bank, she realized that in her nervousness, she had not eaten anything. *It will be OK. I'll pick something up on the way home later,* she thought.

Mary arrived at the bank, and the loan officer was waiting for her. He motioned for her to come in. She walked in, introduced herself, and sat across from him.

"Hi, Mary. It's so nice to meet you." They talked about the inn, and he said that one of his friends had attended a meeting there. "He could not stop talking about the fantastic service the inn provided."

Mary smiled and thanked him for the compliment. "We strive to please our guests," she said.

He already had the application open on his computer and said, "I know this is exciting, your first home and all."

"Yes, it is extremely exciting! This is a dream for sure. The cottage is perfect for me."

"That is great, Mary. I am happy we can be of service to you. This will only take a few minutes. I already have the contract on the house from the Realtor." He began asking her questions about her personal information and financials.

As soon as the application was completed, Mary nervously waited for an answer. She was slightly concerned about her debt-to-income ratio but felt it would be OK, especially since interest rates had dropped and she had excellent credit. She was conscious of how she spent her money and paid her bills on time. She tried hard to be a good steward of what God had provided for her.

The loan officer was doing calculations when he looked up at Mary. He smiled and excused himself. "I'll be right back, Mary. Can I get you anything?"

"No, thank you," said Mary. She was a little anxious about the bank's decision. She wanted the cottage so badly for herself and JJ, but she had prayed for God's will and knew He was with her.

After about ten minutes, he returned to his office and stopped at Mary before going to his desk. He reached out his hand and said, "Mary, congratulations. Your loan has been approved."

She stood up and shook his hand, and before she could catch herself, a tear fell down her cheek. She whispered, "Thank you, Father."

The loan officer told her they had to order a title search and appraisal, but they hired companies that worked only for them, and he said they should have them back in a few days. "Provided they come back good, we should be able to close by the end of the month."

Mary was delighted. She signed the application as needed, thanked him, and said, "I will be looking forward to your call."

As she walked to her car, she felt as if she were going to cry. She couldn't believe her loan was already approved. She picked up her phone to send a group text to her friends: "Girls, I am so excited I could scream! My loan for the cottage was just approved. The bank is ordering an appraisal, and if all goes well, we should be able to move in before the end of the month. Please pray!"

Mary stopped at the local café's drive-through on the way home and picked up a hamburger and french fries. By this time, she was hungry. She knew the hamburger wasn't the best choice, but she didn't care. After all, she had a lot to celebrate. While driving, she decided to eat her lunch to save some time. Just as she finished, she turned into the apartment complex. She pulled into her parking space and thought how nice it would be when they moved. "The ocean will be in my front yard, I can take walks on the beach daily, and so many people love me. I am so blessed," she said.

She walked into the apartment, and JJ was sleeping. She snuggled with him for a minute, sat down, and began writing. Before she realized it, three hours had passed. "You are the sweetest dog in the world," she said. She looked at him and said in a childlike voice, "Do you know how much I love you, JJ?"

It was close to bedtime, and Mary realized she had to give Mr. Henry an answer in the morning about taking the position of general manager. She did not want to break his heart, but she knew the job would give her more responsibility than she wished for. She was enjoying her life now and realized that work should not be the only focus of her life. A balance was necessary, and she felt she had found that balance.

Morning came quickly, and before she knew it, she was back at the office. Mr. Henry met her in her office as she walked in. "Well, Mary, did you decide you would take my job here as general manager?"

"Good morning, Mr. Henry. Wow, you don't even give a girl a chance to get coffee."

"I have a better idea. Let's go get breakfast."

She laughed and said, "That sounds good too."

They walked over, and the hostess greeted them with a warm hello. "You two can be seated wherever you would like." She smiled. They found a private seat in a corner and sat down.

Mr. Henry looked a little sad but anxious.

After their coffee cups were filled and she had a drink, Mary looked at him sadly. "Mr. Henry, you can't even begin to imagine how appreciative I am to you for believing in me and offering your position. I can't think of anyone that could be better at it than you. I don't want to disappoint you, but I hope you understand. I have spent so much of my life since my divorce focusing on work, and it has gotten to the point where work has become my identity. It's different for me now. I have realized that life must have balance. Sure, I would be making a lot more money, but what does that mean? I am blessed to have great friends and a great dog; I love my life. Unfortunately, I can't, Mr. Henry. I am so sorry!"

He looked slightly disappointed but said, "Mary, I understand and am very proud of you. You are exactly right. Life isn't about how much money you can make or the importance of your position if you love it, and I know you love your job. You are great at it, too!"

Mary thanked Mr. Henry for always being understanding and said she would pray that he felt well enough to work for a long time. "Who knows, Mr. Henry? Maybe you will always be my boss. God could heal you; you know."

He smiled and said, "Mary, thank you! You are always so encouraging."

Mary remembered she had yet to tell Mr. Henry about her loan approval for the cottage. She said, "Oh, I can't believe I almost forgot to tell you. My loan was approved to buy the cottage I looked at the other night."

Mr. Henry, in excitement, said, "Mary, that is awesome! Congratulations! Breakfast is on me today." He excused himself and said, "Hold that thought. I will be right back in just a second. I need to check on something quickly."

When he came back, their breakfast had been delivered to the table. They said a prayer and began to eat. After they finished eating, the waitress came over with a chocolate cupcake with buttercream icing. A sparkler was lit on the top. It was pretty.

Mary looked at Mr. Henry and said, "What? Why did you do this?"

He told her congratulations again and winked. "You deserve chocolate for breakfast, Mary."

A tear fell onto her cheek as she realized God had given her the best friends in the world.

Days went by, and she hadn't heard anything from the bank. Mr. Henry was still her boss. He believed in the power of healing and would let God decide his future. He felt sure that He was leading the way.

While Mary was sitting at her desk, reviewing a contract, she got a call from the bank. She took a deep breath and answered.

"Mary, hi. It's Tim at the bank. I received your title search yesterday, and all was clear, but I wanted to wait for the appraisal before I got back to you. I just got the email. Mary, your appraisal came back more than forty thousand dollars over the asking price. Everything is great!"

"Wow," Mary said. "This is excellent news! When can we close?"

"I can have the documents completed whenever you would like. How does Friday sound?"

"Really? That sounds great!"

"How about ten o'clock?"

"Just one second," Mary said. "Let me check my calendar at the office. I don't want to have to move a client. Give me just a minute, please." Mary looked at her calendar, and it was clear for Friday. She returned to the line and said, "My schedule is clear for Friday morning. Oh my goodness! I can't believe this."

Tim told Mary what she needed to bring to the closing.

"Sounds great. Can I start moving in after the closing?"

Tim replied, "You sure can; it will be yours after we close. Congratulations, Mary!"

She thanked him and said, "I'll see you on Friday."

She ran into Mr. Henry's office excitedly. He got up from his desk and said, "Mary, what's wrong?"

She grabbed him, hugged him, and said, "Mr. Henry, I am closing on my cottage Friday morning at ten!"

He grabbed her hand, ran her into the restaurant, and told the hostess, "Please get Mary another cupcake. This time, put two sparklers on it."

Mary looked like a kid when the cupcake came. "You are just too much,

MARTHA GAYLE

Mr. Henry! I love you! Too much chocolate today, though." I will need this one to go. He laughed.

By no coincidence, her lease was to be renewed in thirty days. Mary could not believe how well everything was going.

Mary spent the rest of the morning busy with meetings. She did take a break at lunch and sat in the garden. She found a lot of peace there and went every time she had an opportunity.

She realized she had not texted her friends, so she opened her group chat and texted them: "Girls, I am closing on Friday morning at the bank at 10:00 a.m." The responses came quickly. They were excited for Mary. Karen wanted to know if she was going to try to move some things in on Friday. Mary said the one thing she was sure to move was her favorite writing chair. She was excited about finishing her first book in her new cottage.

Mary would try to get all the utilities connected before the closing on Friday and hoped she didn't have any problems at the closing. She would also pack for the rest of the week in the evenings. She knew she could count on her friends to help, and together, they would get it done.

Mary researched all the required phone numbers for the utility companies and began making the necessary calls. All were scheduled to be turned on early Friday morning.

The rest of the week was busy for Mary. Her days were busy with work, and her evenings consisted of packing. Although she was tired, she enjoyed the packing as she played and sang to her music, and the joy she had was indescribable. Mary was not a great singer, but she didn't care. No one could hear her but Jesus, and He loved to hear her sing.

As she focused on packing, she envisioned herself and JJ in their new home. The thought of being there filled her heart with love. She knew the love was coming from the Lord, as she knew only He could make this dream a reality in her life.

The doorbell rang, and Mary couldn't imagine who was there. She peeped out the window and saw Patricia and Victoria there. They had boxes stacked and plastic containers as well as a bag that looked to contain tacos from the local Mexican restaurant. She opened the door for them, and the laughter she heard was contagious. They all grabbed boxes, and Mary was surprised. She realized she had not had dinner, and the timing was perfect.

24

"Oh, my goodness, girls," Mary said. "What did I do to deserve such great friends? Thank you so much!" Mary asked if they were OK with bottled water, and they both agreed.

As they sat down at the table to eat, Victoria asked if she could pray this time. She thanked the Lord for their food, friendship, and the blessing of knowing they all had one another to go through life with.

Patricia was a beautiful girl and, like Mary, had always wanted to have children and a family. She was also a great Christian girl, and her husband, Paul, was a great leader. He was a youth minister at their church and strived to be a great husband for Patricia.

Victoria was a precious soul. She had been through a lot of adversity in her life, and after trusting and finding hope in her Savior, Jesus Christ, she became a follower. She loved Him and strived to be a better person every day. She loved Mary and was a great friend to her. She had a funny sense of humor that often came out. The girls loved it. They spent a lot of time laughing when she was around.

4

THE CLOSING AND
MOVE-IN DAY

Friday morning came quickly. It was time for Mary to be at the bank for her closing. She had her car packed with as much as she could cram in it. Mary had not had breakfast. She was so nervous that she couldn't eat and had barely slept the night before. This was her first home purchase, and she didn't know what to expect. She had been saving all the extra money she could for a new home, as she knew renting an apartment was not a good investment. Other than the down payment, her mortgage payment would be the same as she was paying in rent, so she felt great about that.

As she walked into the bank, Tim was waiting for her. "Hi, Mary," he said. "Have a seat." He had a stack of papers in front of him. It was a little intimidating to Mary, and she said so. He laughed. "I promise it's not going to be difficult. It just looks like a lot."

"Ha ha," she said.

He asked if he could get her a cup of coffee or something, and she declined. Tim then said, "Let's get started then, if you're ready."

Mary, with a nervous laugh, said, "I am as ready as I will ever be."

After all the paperwork was signed, Tim opened a desk drawer, pulled out the keys to her new cottage, handed them to her, and said, "Mary, congratulations! You are now a homeowner. The lockbox has already been removed from the door, and there is a small gift waiting for you there. It's just a little something to show our appreciation for trusting us to provide you with the service for your loan. Please let me know if I can do anything for you or if you have any questions." He handed her a folder with copies of all the signed documents as well as copies of the title search and appraisal.

Mary took a deep breath and whispered, "Thank you, Lord! You are so good to me! Thank you for making the dream of my new home become a reality. Thank you! Thank you!"

As she arrived at the cottage, she saw three cars parked in the driveway—her friends. As she walked up the cobblestone sidewalk and onto the deck, everyone screamed, "Surprise!" There were balloons everywhere, and a huge sign streaming from the deck said, "Congratulations." The weather was perfect, with not a cloud in the sky. She could hear the ocean waves coming up onto the shore. In her heart, she felt peace and joy that she knew only God could provide.

Victoria then said, "Mary, I hope you don't mind, but while you were at your closing, we took the liberty to pick up the moving truck and take it back to your apartment. It's ready for us there."

Mary was overwhelmed. "You guys are so much more than I deserve. Seriously, what would I do without you?" She threw her hands up, and her new house keys dangled from her fingers.

They told her to go ahead inside.

"You go by yourself. This is your moment, Mary."

She put the key in the door, turned the handle, and walked inside.

The cottage smelled fresh. The painters had been in and touched up all the trim and walls. The cleaners had been in, and everything was perfect.

At once, she noticed a beautifully wrapped gift box sitting on the hearth of the fireplace. She walked over to it and saw it was from the bank. Her first thought was that it was too pretty to open, but she was excited to see what was inside. The girls were right. This was her moment, she thought.

She could hear them talking on the deck, and the sound of their voices made her smile. She felt the love of God from her friends, and at that moment, she needed it. She opened the package, and what was inside brought tears to her eyes. It was a painting of an aerial view of her new cottage with the ocean. It was perfect.

There was a note inside that read,

> Mary, congratulations. We pray your new home is filled with great memories that will last forever. We pray that you'll continue your writings and that many books will be released from those writings. We are waiting to read each one. We haven't spent a lot of time together, as we know this was a business transaction you could have taken anywhere, but we wanted you to know that you inspired us and wanted to say thank you! Blessings to you!
>
> Tim and team

Mary could not believe the kindness of such a gift. As she thought to herself, she said, "There truly is a lot of love in this world, isn't there? Sometimes it seems hard to find, but lately, it has surrounded me, it feels like." Mary wished more people would take the time to look for ways to love others. The world had become dark, it seemed. The last few weeks had been refreshing for her.

Mary felt selfish for being in the house alone for so long and leaving the girls outside. Realizing she had not heard them in a while, she began walking to the door when she realized she had a text. They had left Mary alone on purpose and had gone over to her apartment to begin loading her things. They knew she could get her car unloaded by herself, and getting a head start would be great.

Mary was grateful for the time she spent alone. In the past, taking the time to do these things had been difficult for her. She had matured in her faith and developed greater trust in Jesus. In doing that, she'd stopped striving so much in her own strength and had become freer in her spirit. It seemed to make it easier to stop and take a deep breath as she enjoyed life along the way.

She began unloading her car and putting things away so she could get over to her apartment with the girls. She hoped she and JJ could spend their first night in their new home that night. She picked her phone up to call the girls to see if they had gotten to the apartment yet. Victoria's name was first, so she dialed the number. When Victoria answered, she told Mary they were there and had loaded a lot of what she had packed in the living room. Mary wanted to be sure they'd gotten her favorite chair. They had it, and it was wrapped inside a blanket to keep it from getting any damage.

"Thank you so much, Victoria," Mary said.

After she was done, she grabbed her purse and keys and locked the door behind her. She stood on the deck before leaving and took a deep breath. "Wow! Is this really happening, Lord?" she said. Mary loved the fresh smell of the ocean. She was afraid she was going to wake up from a great dream.

Mary drove through the drive-through and picked up the pizzas she had ordered. She then headed to her apartment to meet the girls. Her thoughts of the kindness of her friends filled her heart with joy. The unselfishness she felt in them was a clear sign that they loved her and were genuinely excited for her.

When she arrived at the apartment, she saw the moving truck backed up at the entrance to her place. She grabbed the pizzas and went inside. Her friends came out of the back of her bedroom, and JJ ran to greet her. She picked him up and said, "Hey, buddy." She told her friends how much she appreciated their hard work and friendship. "You girls are the best! I know it's late, and I haven't even had breakfast, so I picked up some pizzas for all of us."

They all sat down to eat lunch while the pizza was still hot. Mary had water in the refrigerator, so she went to grab a few bottles when she realized they had already completely packed the kitchen. "Oh goodness. You girls haven't wasted any time." Mary thanked them again for their friendship and their help. She told them how grateful she was and that her life would not have been the same without them. "I can't imagine any day of my life without each one of you. You all are a true gift from God."

Mary saw a quick glimpse of the grace of God and His power. *We are not meant to go through life alone. In Galatians 6:2, His Word says, "to carry each other's burdens, and in this way, you will fulfill the law of Christ."* God had certainly put the girls together to do just that, and they all knew it. They were blessed to have one another.

Mary prayed for their meal and thanked Jesus for all He was doing in each of their lives and for all they knew He would continue to do.

They ate every piece of the pizza and found themselves giggling. Patricia said, "We must have been hungry."

Mary said to Patricia, "You may be feeding two now—don't forget."

"I know. I seem to be hungry all the time. May just be hopeful. I don't know. My test last month was negative, so we have decided to test again in a few weeks. Say a prayer for us, please."

Mary told her to be cautious; she had the best job for her. "Will you take care of JJ? We can do the rest."

Patricia didn't feel right about that but agreed. Mary knew JJ needed extra attention with all the moving, so she was happy.

The truck was full midway, and there wasn't much left in the apartment. The boxes were labeled as to the rooms they had come out of, so when they moved them into the cottage, they could place them in the proper rooms. That would help Mary as she unpacked and put everything away.

Mary's phone rang, and it was Mr. Henry. "Mary, congratulations! I wanted to let you know I took the liberty of handling your schedule for this week and next week so you can get settled in your new cottage."

Mary replied, "Are you serious, Mr. Henry? How are you feeling? Thank you so much for that, and I know no one better at handling our clients than you. But you're sick, Mr. Henry and I will never be comfortable putting this pressure on you."

Mr. Henry said that she didn't have a choice and that he would be just fine.

She thanked him and told him, "If you have a chance later, please stop by. It will be a mess, but the Lord sent me a lot of help, and the girls haven't stopped since I opened the door after the closing." She told him they had already rented the moving truck and disappeared from the house when she went inside. "They wanted me to have some time by myself, and I appreciated that so much."

Mr. Henry enjoyed hearing the excitement in Mary's voice and was also grateful for the help she had from her friends.

"This entire day was like a dream, Mr. Henry."

"Mary, you deserve it!" He told her that if he didn't get there that night, he would try hard to get there within a week. "I'll talk to you later, Mary."

Mary said, "I love you, Mr. Henry, and Jesus loves you more than I do."

He said he knew that and replied, "I love you too." The call disconnected.

Mary went through each of the rooms in her apartment, opening cabinets and drawers, looking for anything she had not packed or possibly had forgotten. It had been a busy week with everything going on and packing so late in the night. She was beginning to feel it. But she knew God would give her the strength and great friends to get it all done.

The truck was full, and everything left would fit in Mary's car. They grabbed the last few items and loaded them.

Mary had hired a company to come into the apartment to clean for her. She would check back there after they were done cleaning to be sure it had been cleaned appropriately so she could pay the cleaning company. She always had the desire to leave a place better than she'd found it.

As they arrived back at the cottage, Mary quickly noticed a box on the deck. *That wasn't there when we left*, she thought.

Karen was driving the moving truck, and Victoria was directing her as she backed up. "Stop!" Victoria shouted.

Karen slammed on the brakes just before hitting a palm tree planted to the left of the driveway. She put on the brakes and went out to see what was going on as everyone burst out laughing.

"Karen, girl, you almost took my tree out," Mary said.

"Oh my goodness." Karen began to laugh, too. Karen was embarrassed but quickly got over it because she knew the girls would never let her live it down. Karen wasn't about to move the rented truck except to drive it forward when she had to take it back, so she left it where she'd stopped. They had a few more steps to walk, but she knew that was a better idea, as she was not the best driver when backing up a huge rental truck. She laughed at herself with every added step. This was a moment they would not soon forget.

Mary walked to the gift box on the deck to see who it was from. They all ran over to see what the surprise was. Karen told Mary to hurry and open it. With a kid-like giggle of excitement, Mary opened the box. It was a doormat and was personalized. It read, "Mary's Cottage by the Sea. Welcome." She began to cry and wondered who it was from.

As she tipped the box, a note fell out onto the deck. She picked it up and read,

> Mary, congratulations. I pray your new cottage brings you much love and joy and is a peaceful, happy place for you and JJ—a place for you to write excellent books that everyone in the world will want to read.
>
> Signed,
> Mr. Henry

Mary almost couldn't catch her breath. She loved Mr. Henry and quickly thought of their conversations about his sickness. She began to pray. "Lord, thank you again for my friend. Please, Lord, heal his body for your glory. Thank you, Lord, for bringing him into my life. He's a special person, and I need him. In Jesus's name, amen."

Mary was always there for everyone else and was having trouble receiving all that God was giving her. She was grateful and continued to ask the Lord to help her receive His love in humility.

Patricia asked Mary if she could walk JJ out on the beach. Mary responded, "Sure. He will love it."

Karen and Victoria began unloading the truck and bringing her things inside the house. They tried to place everything in the proper rooms, except for many items Mary would stack in the guest bedroom, as she didn't have furniture yet and wanted to keep it all organized.

Finally, the truck and her car were unloaded, and they were all exhausted. It was getting late, so they decided to get her bed put together so she would have her bed to sleep in. She had put a couple of changes of clothes and supplies in a separate bag for the next couple of days of unpacking, as well as her sheets and blankets for her bed. She also had JJ's toys, food, and snacks in a separate bag. She kept everything close to her, as she knew they would need it.

Karen went into the refrigerator and pulled out a bottle of chardonnay she had purchased for them to celebrate. She had small, clear plastic cups as well. She called them all to the kitchen after pouring the wine. They all laughed and grabbed cups. As they toasted Mary and JJ for happiness in her new cottage, they talked about the day and how well it had gone.

Mary said, "Yeah, apart from Karen almost running into my palm tree." They laughed hysterically.

Victoria decided it was time to get home. Paul was waiting for her, as they always tried to spend time together each evening to discuss their days and have prayer time. They all agreed it was time to wrap it up for the night.

After the girls left, Mary looked at JJ and said, "Hey, buddy, come here. Mom needs some love from you." He ran over, and she picked him up. "Well, what do you think? Can you believe we are in our new home? It's a mess right now." She walked into the kitchen, picked up his bag, and pulled out his food, water bowls, and mat. "Let's get you something to eat, buddy. Mom's sorry it's so late. This has been a great day, but I am exhausted." She left her outside floodlights on, locked the door, and entered her bedroom.

Mary grabbed her bag and pulled out her shampoo, conditioner, body wash, towel, and washcloth. She then jumped into the shower and put on her pajamas. JJ looked uncertain about where he was, but he knew Mary was there, so he stayed close to her.

She then put her sheets and quilt on her bed with pillows and grabbed her journal, and they both crawled into bed. She began to write about her day. After writing, she looked at her leather carry bag on a table beside the bed, which held her manuscript and laptop for her new book. The thought of almost being finished with her manuscript made her happy. She was excited that she would finish writing it at her new cottage.

Mary looked down at her phone. She'd received messages from Victoria, Karen, and Patricia. They had all made it home safely. JJ snuggled beside her. She said her prayers and then drifted to sleep.

5

SETTLING IN

Morning came quickly. The sun was shining through the window, and Mary realized it was already seven o'clock. JJ was still sleeping. She looked over at him and thanked Jesus for him. She had missed him yesterday, but he loved spending time with Patricia. She was grateful Patricia had spent the day looking after him, so she didn't have to worry. She needed to focus on getting everything moved. She was also grateful to Karen and Victoria for helping her. She realized it would have taken her weeks to get the move done without them.

As she got up and threw her robe on, she realized she had no idea where her coffeepot was. "Oh no, JJ, Mom needs her coffee. Wonder where my coffeepot is." Mary had packed her coffeepot and had no idea where to find it. "The sound of the ocean is wonderful this morning, JJ," said Mary. "We are going to be so happy here."

As they came back in, she heard her phone ringing. It was Victoria. "Hey," Victoria said. I am on my way to run some errands. How was your night?"

Mary replied that it had been great. "I don't think I moved after I fell asleep. JJ and I slept until seven this morning."

"Wow, that's great," said Victoria.

Mary laughed and said, "I feel in such disarray. I can't find my coffeepot."

Victoria laughed and said, "Well, we both know that's not going to work for you, don't we?" Victoria said that on her way out, she would stop by Joe's Coffee to pick up an extra-large cup for Mary.

Mary replied, "You are awesome! Thank you! I desperately need coffee this morning."

Mary fed JJ and began looking at the labels on some of her boxes. She was happy to be in her new home and knew she would get it organized soon enough. She felt she could take her time and was grateful to Mr. Henry for giving her so much time off.

Mary sat down to read her Bible for a few minutes. She knew she needed His presence daily and knew how important it was for her to start her day that way. She quoted silently in her mind the words in 2 Timothy 3:16–17: "All Scripture is God-breathed and is useful for teaching, rebuking, correcting, and training in righteousness. So that the servant of God may be thoroughly equipped for every good work." She also thought of Psalm 119:105: "Your word is a lamp to my feet, a light on my path." God's Word was a lamp to Mary's feet, and she was continuing to learn how important it was to stay focused on Jesus, or she would be a mess.

She was comfortably sitting in her favorite chair when Victoria rang the doorbell. Mary went to the door. Victoria had an extra-large cup of coffee with cream and Anderson's pure maple syrup in her hand, just as Mary liked it. It was hot, and it was perfect. She hugged Victoria, and they sat down for a minute.

Victoria looked around and said to Mary, "You've got a mess," and she laughed. She wanted to stay to help her but knew she couldn't. She had a day full of errands and knew she would pay for it later if she didn't get them done.

Mary was happy to spend the day alone with JJ. She knew where to put everything, and she would take her time. She thought they might even walk on the beach a little later. "Maybe, after I get just a little more organized, I can try to get closer to finishing my book." Mary said the publisher was waiting for the manuscript. "The move has put me behind." She felt peace, realizing it would all work out just as it was supposed to.

Mary spent four hours going through her boxes and putting things away. She had just about finished her kitchen, and she'd put away all her groceries last night before bed. Mary had not shopped for groceries the previous week, as she had known she would be moving.

She finally found her coffeepot and was happy about that. She did a little dance in the kitchen and giggled at herself. Mary loved coffee, so that was a priority.

She felt hungry and went into the pantry to find her oatmeal. Her pots and pans were in the sink to be washed from the move. She quickly grabbed a small pot, washed it, measured two cups of reverse-osmosis-filtered water, and put the pot on a burner on her cooktop. *Oatmeal sounds good this morning*, she thought. Mary loved oatmeal with granola, organic dried cranberries, a dash of cinnamon, and her favorite pure maple syrup. *This is perfect*, she thought. The oatmeal hit the spot, and Mary was ready for the day ahead. She was happy and even loved seeing the mess of boxes stacked everywhere.

The morning went quickly. Mary decided to take a break and get some fresh air. "Hey, JJ, let's go for a walk on the beach." He was happy to explore. "Maybe we will collect a few seashells."

She changed from her pajamas and wore a pair of sweatpants and a sweatshirt. The temperatures were still slightly cool in the mornings. She grabbed JJ's leash and called him to go outside. They went out the door, and she locked it behind her.

Mary thought to herself, *I can't believe this isn't a dream.* Before they knew it, they were on the sand. Seashells were everywhere. As they walked, she would occasionally stop and look down to see if one spoke to her heart. Something about a seashell warmed her heart in a fun way. She thought; *They are all so unique, like all of God's children. We are none alike, but God uses all of us to show love and care for one another.*

Mary was happy to be in her new cottage. It was a beautiful day. Mary realized God had used her to take JJ, but JJ had rescued her. Realizing he was a gift from God, she whispered a prayer and said, "Thank you, Jesus, for my new friend. My heart is so full."

After walking, Mary thought they had better get back to the cottage. She still had more work to do and wanted to write a little more of her book before the day was over. She was getting close to finishing the manuscript.

She could feel herself getting tired throughout the day, as yesterday had been nonstop. She could tell her body was sore from the move, but she knew the exercise was good for her.

They walked a few minutes longer and decided it was time to turn back to walk toward the cottage. After they got inside, JJ got a drink of water and found his bed in the sun by the window to lie down.

Mary chose her favorite music on her phone, increased the volume, and began going through more boxes and putting things away. She was enjoying it, as she had hoped this would be their home for a long time. Moving was not her favorite thing to do, but this time, it felt different. It felt special. She felt she was finally at home. Then, before she realized it, it was lunchtime. She needed to go to the grocery store to pick up a few things.

Mary decided to jump in the shower. She loved her tile shower, and the pebble floor felt great on her feet. She hadn't realized the showerhead had an adjustable massager. *Wow,* she thought, *this is nice.* The water pressure was incredible. Her muscles were sore. She couldn't believe how hard they had pushed themselves the day before. She was there longer than she wanted, but the warm water and the showerhead massager felt great on her sore back and shoulders.

When she came out of the shower, she saw JJ lying on a rug in the bathroom, waiting for her. She realized he was a little uncomfortable, not fully understanding what was happening with the move. She picked him up and cuddled him to reassure him that all would be OK.

Mary decided that day would be a quick outing, so she put her favorite ball cap on and decided not to wear makeup. She then grabbed her purse and keys and walked out the door. While driving to the store, on the right, off Sunnyside Lane, she saw a nice dog park called Fun-Park. It looked like a lot of fun, Mary thought. There were many dogs out playing with their moms and dads. She saw automatic water feeders in the center. Some were raised higher than others—she guessed for different heights of dogs. Mary thought she needed to take JJ there sometime. *Maybe tomorrow will be a good day. He would love that,* she thought.

Her phone rang, and it was Mr. Henry. He had a question about one of her clients. They discussed it for a few minutes, and then he asked her how the move had gone. She couldn't quit talking about the girls and how much help they had been.

With everything going on, she almost forgot to tell him how much she loved her doormat. "Mr. Henry, you are one of the most beautiful people I have ever met. I cried when I opened my gift yesterday. It's perfect! Thank you so much!" Mary then asked Mr. Henry how he was feeling.

He told her about the treatments he was using and how much more energy he had. He was amazed. "I have a feeling you are right, Mary. God may heal this old body and keep me around a little longer. I pray He does for sure, and I will give Him all the glory. It will be His decision. We both know that don't we?"

Mr. Henry told Mary he had wanted to stop by the cottage to see it that day, but he was busy and thought he would get by there in a few days for sure. He would come by as soon as he could.

Mary arrived at the grocery store, and Mr. Henry was ready to say goodbye. She thanked him again for the time off work and said, "You knew I needed it more than I did. I can't imagine balancing all this and being at the inn all day. You have made this so much easier for me. I love you, Mr. Henry."

"I love you back, Mary! Call me if you need anything." They hung up.

Mary went into the grocery store and grabbed a cart. She planned to get a few things and get in and out quickly. She went down the produce aisle and picked up some fresh fruit. Mary loved fruit. She grabbed some red potatoes, brussels sprouts, asparagus, and cabbage. She knew that with all the pizza and hamburgers she had eaten, she had better return to something healthy. She went down the meat aisle and thought about a nice fillet. They were on sale, so she picked up a couple. She loved the Amish brand chicken breast and saw it was also on sale, so she picked up three packages and thought she could put some in the freezer. Mary remembered JJ's food and went down the aisle to pick it up. They were out of his favorite snacks, so she found another kind she would try for him. She quickly ran through the store, picked up a few additional items, and headed to the checkout.

As she walked to the checkout, she glanced at the coffee shop and thought coffee sounded good. Only a couple of people were in line, so she set her cart aside and waited. She finally placed her order, and the young barista handed her the coffee. With her first sip, Mary thought, *That's exactly what I needed.*

Mary got in line to pay for her groceries when she realized the self-checkouts were all full. As she looked around the store a bit, she saw a young cashier waiting at the end of the line to help someone.

Mary quickly walked that way, pushing her basket, and began getting her groceries out of the cart. She looked up at the young girl, who looked as if she had been crying. Mary didn't say anything at first but whispered a prayer for her. When she finished putting her groceries on the counter, she asked the girl how she was that day.

The cashier looked down and said, "I'm good. How about you?"

Mary knew she wasn't telling the truth. She could feel it. She looked at her name tag: Tiffany. Mary started small talk and told her that Jesus loved her. Tiffany glanced up at her with a strange look. Mary wanted to be her friend and encourage her but didn't know how to handle it in line at the grocery store.

Before leaving the checkout, Mary pulled out her business card and quickly wrote her cell number on the back of it. She handed it to Tiffany and said, "I know you don't know me, and I understand if you don't call, but I want you to know I'm a great listener, and I would love to be your friend."

Tiffany took the card and smiled. She said, "Thank you."

Mary left with her groceries.

Tiffany stayed on Mary's mind a lot that day. She continued to pray for her as she put her groceries away. Then she washed her hands, made a quick sandwich, and sat in her chair to write. The sun was coming through the window, giving her the right amount of light.

Mary could hear the ocean waves, and even with boxes sitting around the room, she couldn't imagine being any happier.

When she looked at her phone to see the time, Mary did not realize how long she had been writing. She had been sitting there for more than three hours, and the last words written were "To be continued." Mary had finished her manuscript. She sat there with her laptop in her lap and prayed. "Father, this story has made me cry and laugh, and I have enjoyed writing it so much. Thank you for this opportunity you have given me. Father, I pray the words in my book will touch the hearts of many as you draw them to yourself. You gave me these words; I will give them to you now. May your will be done. In Jesus's name, I pray. Amen."

Mary opened her email and composed a message to her publisher:

> You will never believe what happened today. I have finished the manuscript for my book. I am attaching it here. Please let me know if you need anything else. I look forward to hearing back on the next steps with the editorial process and an estimated time of publication. Thank you for helping me to make this dream a reality.
>
> Blessings,
> Mary

She hit send, sat back in her chair, took a deep breath, and said, "It's all yours from here, Lord."

It was getting late, and Mary wanted a home-cooked meal. She pulled out a package of the chicken she had gotten at the grocery store and decided to bake it with lemon garlic butter and fresh parsley. She pulled out a few pieces of her asparagus, diced some potatoes, and decided that would be a great dinner.

As her dinner was baking, she fed JJ and walked over to the window. As she stared out over the ocean, she thought of her book. She wondered how long it would take to do the edits and what the artwork would look like on the cover. *This is very exciting*, she thought. Her next thought made her realize that all the efforts in writing the story would be worth it if only one person came to know Jesus. She smiled and said, "Father, help me to relax. I have given you this book now and am excited about how you will turn it all out. Help me leave it in your hands and enjoy the journey you have given me. In Jesus's name, amen."

Mary reached for the table to pick up her phone and realized she had missed a call from Karen. Before listening to the voice mail, she hit the call button. Karen was checking on her to see how her day had been. Mary told her what she had done and how she'd found the time to write.

Karen was surprised to hear she had finished the manuscript and had emailed it to the publisher. "Wow," said Karen, "I'm happy I left you alone today, Mary. You have gotten a lot done." Karen then asked how JJ was doing and how he was adjusting to their new home.

"He's doing great if I am close to him. He doesn't leave my side very much, though. He will be fine, I'm sure."

Mary then asked Karen how she was doing and if she was sore from all the moving yesterday. Karen laughed and said, "Yes, I am. I thought I was in better shape but realize I need to spend a lot more time doing strength exercises."

Mary agreed they both did, and they giggled. Mary thanked Karen again and said, "We should get together for dinner this weekend. We can meet here if you would like. I'll try to get these boxes unpacked." She then said she would text the group chat to see if everyone was available for Saturday afternoon.

Karen said, "That sounds great, Mary. It will be fun!" They agreed they would talk later and hung up.

Mary spent the rest of the evening unpacking a few boxes. She liked the way it all was coming together.

Before she knew it, it was time for bed. She changed into her pajamas, crawled into bed, prayed, and drifted to sleep.

Morning came quickly. She had no plans for her day and liked it that way. She was enjoying her time off, taking in the move and not feeling rushed to unpack. Mr. Henry had been a blessing to her in giving her the time off. She had not asked for it, and the time off from work was a fantastic gift.

Mary climbed out of bed and turned on her coffee to brew. She filled her coffee cup and then decided to sit on the deck for a few minutes while she sipped her coffee. While sitting there, she realized she needed a new set of deck furniture and thought that it might be a great day to shop. She then thought about the dog park and how nice it would be to take JJ there for a while.

Mary walked back inside and sat in her favorite chair to read her Bible. She reminded herself, *This is a priority, and Jesus always needs to come first.* She bowed her head and began to pray. "Father, only you know my plans for today. I ask that you fill me with your spirit so that my day is filled with your peace and joy, no matter what comes my way."

After praying and reading, Mary made a quick breakfast and decided it was the perfect time to take JJ to the new dog park. She quickly got up and dressed. "Let's go, buddy," she said. "I have a surprise for you today. Thank you for being such a good boy."

The park was only a few minutes from the cottage, so the drive was short. She found a parking place and saw only a few dogs there. She grabbed JJ's leash, and they walked into the park. It only took him about two minutes to find a friend.

Mary looked down and saw a cute Lab puppy standing next to her. When she looked up to see who was on the other end of the leash, she took a deep breath. The moment felt a little awkward when a tall, handsome man reached out a hand and said, "Hi. I'm David."

Mary was a little surprised, and before she knew it, she was saying, "Hi. I'm Mary."

David began talking about how nice the dog park was and said he had never seen her there. He told her that Remi, the Lab puppy, wasn't his; he was dog-sitting for a friend. Mary said she had never been there before and was happy she had found the park.

Mary knew JJ would enjoy playing with new friends. JJ began pulling on the leash as if to say he was ready to play, so she told David it was nice meeting him and walked away.

Mary found an area for small dogs of his size that was privately fenced, walked inside, and closed the gate. She then found a bench to sit on, took his leash off, and let him run. He was having so much fun, running around and playing with the other dogs there. She'd brought a book with her but thought she had better keep an eye on him this time until they got used to the park.

In just a few minutes, David came over to where she was and asked if he could sit with her. Mary agreed, and he sat down. Mary had been enjoying herself without him but didn't want to be rude. He began talking to her about the weather and said he wasn't looking forward to the winter. Mary agreed that she didn't like the winter either and wished the seasons could skip to the spring.

He laughed. "That would be great if we could make that happen," he said.

They spent about an hour talking when David asked Mary for her phone number. It caught her off guard, but before she knew it, she had written it down and handed it to him. She quickly called JJ, and after he ran over to her, she connected his leash and told David it was nice to meet him, and they both walked away.

Mary had surprised herself by giving David her number and thought she wished to take it back. As she drove home, she began to pray. "Father, please protect me. In Jesus's name, amen."

They arrived at the cottage, and JJ found his bed and lay down. He was tired after all the playing that morning. Mary made herself some lemon water and sat down to check her emails. She had an email from her publisher. It read,

> Mary, the editing of your book is complete, and the artwork on the cover is being finalized. We will send you the artwork for your approval soon. It should be in the next couple of days. We have already presented a preliminary copy of your book to retailers to get an estimated number for the first print. I can tell you that you will be pleased. We will discuss those numbers with you after we get the final figures. Your book is going to sell very well, Mary. We are very excited for you. I will be back in touch soon!
>
> Johnathon

Mary had many thoughts going through her head. She reread the email and stopped at the line "I think you will be pleased." She dropped to her knees and began to pray. "Father, I am feeling very anxious. Please give me peace. You already know how this book will sell, and I am very excited. Help me, Lord, to stay humble and continue giving you my anxious heart so I may receive your peace. It is yours, Lord, and I pray that you are most glorified. Please help me not to take it back, as I have already given it to you. Thank you, Father, for your amazing love. In Jesus's name, I pray. Amen."

When Mary got up, she felt peace once again. She knew she needed to unpack boxes and wanted to go shopping later for patio furniture. She spent a couple of hours unpacking.

She had boxes stacked that needed to be thrown away, and she realized the recycling center was only a few blocks away. She didn't know how many she could get in her car, but she knew it would be easier if she tried to break them down. So, she walked out onto the deck, began breaking down the empty boxes, and decided she would take them on the way out to shop for the furniture. It took her about thirty minutes, but when they were all broken down, she thought she could get most of them in her car. After she was done, she made herself a quick sandwich and headed out.

Mary put the address of the recycler in her GPS and began driving. It only took her a few minutes to get there. She unloaded all the boxes and changed her GPS to directions for the furniture store.

Finally, she arrived, and outdoor furniture was lined up everywhere. She saw all the different colors and designs. She knew what she was looking for and would know as soon as she saw it. Mary exited the car, locked it behind her, and began browsing. She saw it as she turned a corner in the store: a perfect white table made of Polywood with four matching chairs. The umbrella was sold separately, but she felt she needed to get one in case the summer sun was too hot. The price was marked down by more than 20 percent. Mary thought it was the perfect time to purchase a patio set. She was happy about the sale. She found the ideal umbrella and base and told the sales associate she would take all six pieces. The store agreed to deliver all for a fifty-dollar fee. Mary felt relieved that she had finally gotten the set she needed, and she paid the bill and set up the delivery arrangements.

This has been a great day, Mary thought. Going out and shopping had given her a break from all the moving and unpacking. She was excited to be buying important pieces she knew would provide a lot of happy memories with others. The balance she was finding in her life was refreshing.

6

THE CELEBRATION

D riving back to her cottage, Mary had thoughts about her day and wanted to spend some time writing but knew it would be almost impossible. She was continuing to get more settled in her new cottage, and it felt great. The peace she felt there was indescribable. The sunlight brightened the rooms with a warmth that was always welcome. Mary had grown to love JJ so much. He had become a great companion and she knew he was a precious gift from God.

Mary adored her cottage, and when she wasn't busy with other things, she spent much of her spare time decorating to make it even more inviting. She loved fresh flowers and usually had a bouquet on her kitchen table. They always seemed to bring a feeling of renewal.

Mary decided she would make a cup of coffee to give herself a boost for the afternoon and take a walk on the beach. She loved searching for seashells and usually stumbled across at least one seashell she loved. She always wondered how far the shells had traveled. Heart-shaped shells were rare but were always her favorite. When she found one, it always made her smile, and she accepted them as gifts from God. She had started a collection of them and put them on a table by the front door. They all had a story, and most had meanings, as occasionally God would encourage her through them.

The rooms were all filled with unique pieces of art collected through the years. They meant a lot to her. She had an excellent eye for detail that brought her back to the reality of her life.

The timer on her phone rang to remind her that the brownies she'd made were ready to come out of the oven. Mary loved chocolate and found it hard to resist most of the time. For some reason, chocolate comforted her. Her friends were coming over for dinner to celebrate her new beginnings in her new home. Later, she was going to prepare her favorite pasta. The girls were bringing over other dishes they had prepared, and she knew they would be perfect. Their time together was always special, and the excitement of her first book about to be published was almost unmanageable.

Mary was getting anxious to hear back from the publisher. She wondered when she would start writing her second book, as she knew exactly how it would start. *I will take a short break*, she thought, but she already missed writing.

Mary jumped into the shower and towel-dried her hair. She decided to leave it natural that day, and she put on her makeup. She then put on jeans, a cute top with beautiful coral-colored flowers with green leaves, and a cardigan sweater. As she thought about the shoes she would wear, she looked in her closet and found her favorite flats. She was adorable and was looking forward to the celebration. Her friends meant so much to her; having them there with her to celebrate was a blessing to Mary. They all had different personalities that blended well together, and Mary thanked God for her friends.

The phone rang, and it was Karen. She wanted to come by a little early so she could talk to Mary about something. Mary, of course, told her that would be fine.

When Karen arrived, she looked a little concerned. Mary welcomed her in, and they sat outside on the deck. Karen told Mary that Sam wanted her to leave her career, as he felt it was too stressful for her, and when they had children, he wanted her to be a stay-at-home wife and mom. He thought her leaving now would allow them enough time to get adjusted to only one income and would also give her time to get used to being at home. They wanted to try to have a baby soon, but she wasn't ready to leave her career. Karen worked at an advertising agency and had been there for five years.

She loved her job and couldn't imagine her life without it. "What would I do all day long?" she said. Karen had a legitimate concern, but Sam also had a great point.

Mary asked Karen how soon they planned to have children and how she felt about being a stay-at-home wife and mom. Karen told Mary they were trying now to get pregnant but had not had any luck in several months. She also shared that she had never thought about staying home, because she had never thought of giving up her career at the ad agency. She did have an interest in homeschooling if it was God's will that they have children. Mary understood her point but reassured her that, as a couple, they would work it out together. Mary held Karen, told her it would be OK, and asked if she could pray with her. She knew Karen's heart and knew she could be a little dramatic at times as well, but this time, she had legitimate concerns. The decision was important to Karen, and Mary took it seriously.

As she held her hand, Mary began to pray. "Father, we come to you today to ask for your presence to surround us. Father, as Karen feels her husband is leading her to leave her career, I pray, Lord, that you comfort her. Help them, Lord, together to make a unified decision that both are comfortable with as they ask you to lead them. As a married couple, may they be unified in you and follow your will. Father, as they are also trying to get pregnant and build a family, I pray that you fill their hearts with your peace, and your will be done. In Jesus's name, amen."

Mary looked over at Karen with a sweet smile and said, "I remember a moment in my life a few years ago when God called me to follow Him in a decision that was difficult for me too. I trusted Him all the way till Wednesday. God showed up on Thursday, Karen. You can trust Him." The look on Karen's face was priceless. God's joy and peace surrounded her. Mary hugged her friend and said, "It's all going to be OK."

They were reminded of Galatians 6:2–5: "Bear ye one another's burdens and so fulfill the law of Christ."

"Now, let's get ready for our celebration!"

They walked into the kitchen to start putting the prepared food out on the bar. Mary had fresh flowers on the table. It all looked amazing. Mary said, "It is almost time for the girls to arrive." Before she could get the words out, the doorbell rang. Patricia and Victoria were at the door with big smiles and a bouquet of balloons.

"Your cottage is perfect! Look how much you have gotten done, Mary. It looks like you've been here for a long time."

They all laughed, remembering the move-in day and how hard they'd pushed themselves.

The girls all poured glasses of homemade lemonade Mary had made and began to talk. The excitement in the room was contagious. They made a toast to life's greatest accomplishments. Mary said with a warm smile, "Look what God has done and is doing in all our lives." Joy filled each of their hearts, and the sound of laughter from everyone made her smile. "This is going to be an amazing day, girls. Thank you so much for coming. God has blessed me with each of you."

They all walked out onto the deck and talked for a while. They talked about the fun times they'd had at Mary's apartment and how much they were looking forward to more great times at the cottage for years to come. Her new patio table was great, and they all loved sitting outside. The sound of the ocean waves was refreshing and brought a feeling of peace.

After about thirty minutes of their sharing and encouraging one another, Mary asked if they were all ready to eat. Everyone said, "Yes!" with excitement. They all made their plates and walked back outside to eat.

Mary said a prayer over their food. "Father, thank you for my friends. Thank you for the love you bring me through each one of them. I can't imagine my life without you or any of them. Thank you for this food. Please use it to nourish our bodies, and may we continue to do life together as you bring glory to yourself. In Jesus's name, amen."

The pasta was fantastic. Victoria had made a beautiful salad, and Patricia had brought over homemade bread and a special oil with seasoning for dipping. She was an amazing breadmaker. Everything tasted delightful. They sat around and talked for hours when they realized it was getting dark.

The temperatures were getting cooler in the mid-fifties. Mary had a gas firepit installed in the yard just off the deck, with four chairs surrounding it. Mary suggested they go out and try her new firepit. She said, "I haven't had time to use it yet, and what a great way to break it in with the best friends in the world." They all ran off the deck, giggling like small kids. Mary turned on the firepit, and it only took a couple of minutes to warm them up. They decided to talk about their childhoods and how good God had been to each one of them.

Victoria was a serious person and had a beautiful personality. She had thin blonde hair with bangs combed over to the left. She was a special friend to Mary. As she started talking about her life and how she was continuing to grow in the Lord, she had everyone's attention. She shared that she had accepted the Lord as her Savior as a young adult.

Victoria had not had the privilege of growing up in a home with Jesus's love. Life had been tough for her as a child. Her dad had been disabled and unable to work. He had not chosen his words correctly as he spoke down to her instead of building her up, and she had grown up insecure and lonely. Her mom had always worked to provide for the family. After Victoria had come to Christ, her dad also accepted Jesus into his life. Life had been different for her after that. She had been happy for her dad, and the family had finally found unity. He'd begun to pray with them every day, and the Lord had reconciled the past unforgiveness and pain.

Victoria finally understood what it meant to depend on the love and grace of Jesus, and she had found joy that no one could take away. She was happy. Her husband, John, was a good man. He loved Victoria, and it was clear in his character. They had met in college and had been through a lot together. Through struggles, they were learning what it took to have a happy marriage, and Jesus was the center of their lives.

Patricia was a beautiful girl. She'd married her high school sweetheart, Paul. She had long, straight auburn hair. She was tall and slim, and everyone loved her. Her life growing up was the opposite of Victoria's. Her family had always attended church every Sunday, and she had always gone to youth meetings as well as church camp every summer. She'd accepted Jesus as her Lord and Savior and had been saved at a young age.

Patricia's dad had been a deacon in the church. Their life had looked beautiful on the outside to everyone who knew them, but she'd had many secrets that caused a lot of distrust and unbelief in her life. Her dad had not been nice to her mom, and she had always had to step up for her mom. That had brought much division into their home. When Patricia was an older teen, after a tragic accident, her dad accepted the Lord in his life and began to follow God's guidance in leading their home.

Patricia's mom had been grateful for who he had become as their lives had changed. She was happy she had never given up on their marriage. It finally had become beautiful and unified, as she had always imagined it would be. Patricia ended her talk by saying, "God made my mom and dad's marriage beautiful."

Karen's childhood had been peaceful growing up. Her dad had prayed with the family every day and led by the example of Jesus's love. Karen remembered how nurturing her mom had been, and the smell of freshly baked bread and meals had always filled the home. Karen had received her baking skills from her mom, as they had always baked together. She had always felt the example of God's love through her parents. When disappointments had come, and they had, her daddy had always held her, prayed with her, and reminded her that Jesus was nearby. Her life had pain, but she knew where to go to find the answers and peace. She went to Jesus!

Karen was blessed; she knew many of her friends hadn't had what she had while growing up, and she always tried to encourage them. Karen had been popular in school and had overseen the school newspaper, as well as being chosen as valedictorian of her class. She desired to love everyone and prayed daily for her friends.

The evening was relaxing, and the girls felt close to Jesus and one another. The time together was rewarding for each of them. Sharing their lives together was a gift from God, and they all knew it. Mary thought of Mark 5:19: "Go home to your friends and tell them what wonderful things the Lord has done for you and how merciful He has been."

The girls talked for hours, laughing at one another's stories. There were times when they cried together and prayed for one another. God blessed Mary with amazing friends. They were all real and transparent, and she always enjoyed spending time with each one. She knew in her heart they were a gift from the Lord, and Mary thanked Him continuously for their love for her, as well as her love for them.

It was almost eleven when Mary said, "Oh my goodness, girls, it is almost eleven. We had so much fun that we totally had no idea it had gotten so late. Maybe we'd better wrap this up until another day." As they got up and gathered their things, Mary turned off the gas on the firepit, and they walked inside to pick up their dishes to leave.

"Give me hugs," Mary said. "What great fun we had tonight. Thank y'all so much! I needed that! Let's do this more often." They all agreed. Mary made it a point to make time for moments like these, as they were important, she thought.

As she got back inside, she immediately thought of John 15:13: "Greater love has no one than this, to lay down one's life for one's friends." She knew God had given her friends who would be there for her no matter what, and they had proven that. She also wanted to be that kind of friend for them as well.

Mary understood the sacrifice the girls had gone through to help her get moved into her cottage. She knew it wasn't something they'd had to do, but they had made a choice to serve her as a friend, and Mary prayed she never took their friendship for granted.

After climbing into bed, Mary realized she had texts from the girls: they had all made it home safely. It was always important to Mary that they texted her, so she didn't worry about them. She realized she also had another text. "Who is this from? I wonder," said Mary.

The text read, "Hi, Mary. It's David. We met at the dog park yesterday. I wondered if you would be interested in going out to dinner on Friday night. It was so nice meeting you, and I would love to get to know you better."

Mary had to read it again. She didn't know if she was ready to date again, and the thought of it made her uncomfortable. After all, she was happy with her life right now, just as it was. She laid her phone down, prayed, snuggled with JJ, and drifted off to sleep.

Mary woke up, realizing she had not slept well. She'd tossed and turned throughout the night and had strange dreams. She couldn't imagine what had been on her mind when she recalled David's text asking her out.

Memories of Edward went through her mind, and she didn't know if she was ready for dating yet. She prayed that God would help her have peace if this was something He thought she should do.

Her morning routine was the same: getting JJ outside to go potty, drinking her coffee as she read her Bible, spending time with the Lord, and taking a walk on the beach. She loved her routine and knew it would change when she had to go back to work.

That morning felt different for some reason. She thought a dinner date would be good for her, so she picked up her phone and replied to David's text: "Hi, David. Good morning. Thank you for the dinner invite. I have a busy schedule, but let's go to dinner. Tomorrow night would work well if that's OK with you."

He responded quickly. "Great, Mary. I'm looking forward to it. Is six too early?"

Mary agreed that six would be fine, and she felt a little excited. *A date, huh?* she said to herself. *Well, I guess a new friend is always good.*

Mary had not dated in what seemed like forever and didn't know if she was ready. Her divorce from Edward had given her many feelings of uncertainty and distrust.

7

NEW FRIENDS

As the temperatures were dropping, Mary was preparing her heart for a lot of time indoors and starting on her next book. JJ was always wonderful company for her. A winter by the sea would be perfect for writing. Mary sat in her favorite chair, sipping a cup of lemon ginger tea and watching the waves crash against the shore. She began to pray. "Father, thank you! Thank you again for my beautiful cottage. Thank you for the power that lives inside me. You are my source, my life, and my freedom. Lord, as I begin to write today, I pray that your words be written. I pray that in your words, you touch the hearts of many and draw them to yourself. I pray they receive you as their Lord and Savior. So many are wondering today in a world filled with chaos and feel they have no hope, having no idea, Father, that you are our hope, our joy, and our greatest gift. You are the Alpha and the Omega, the beginning and the end. May hearts be filled with joy and your salvation today. In Jesus's name, I pray. Amen."

After hours of sitting in her chair, writing, Mary realized it was close to three in the afternoon. Time had gotten away from her, and she had a dinner date at six. David was picking her up at the cottage. He had made reservations at a romantic Italian restaurant on the island, where a live jazz band always played in the background. The food was always superb there, and he must have been listening when they first met because they had talked about their favorite foods. She felt surprisingly excited. David was a handsome man, tall and blond, and had a great personality.

This was their first date, and Mary realized she was interested in hearing more about him and getting to know him better. Mary was nervous but knew God was with her.

Mary jumped into the shower, slipped on her robe, and dried her hair. She decided to use her curling iron. She could add some loose curls to soften the frame of her face. She applied makeup. Mary didn't wear makeup often, only when company was coming over or when she was going out. It always made her feel good to dress up a bit. Mary loved sweatpants and T-shirts when she was at home. Being comfy was always a priority for her.

She walked into the closet, deciding what to wear, and she picked out a cute light blue top made of linen fabric, navy dress jeans, and her favorite shoe boots. She was happy about her choice.

The phone rang. It was Karen.

"Hi, Karen. How are you?"

"I'm great, Mary. How are you?"

"I am excited and nervous, haha. David is picking me up for dinner in a little while. We are going to the Italian restaurant that you and I went to for lunch a couple of months ago."

"That sounds fun, Mary. Don't be nervous; relax and enjoy his company. Take it slow, and be his friend. Jesus will lead you.

"I have some great news! I am putting my resignation in on Monday. Sam and I have decided we are going to trust the Lord. I'm so excited! I know we will have trials, and there will be times when we are afraid, but we both feel this is the right choice for us."

"Karen, that is awesome! You will have trials, but you are making the right decision. I just know it! Let's plan a time soon to get together. We all had so much fun the other day, celebrating my new home." They agreed and hung up quickly as David was at the door.

As the doorbell rang a second time, Mary ran to the door. David stood there with a bouquet of beautiful flowers—a welcome surprise for a cold winter day. She put the flowers in a vase and said thank you with a smile. Mary grabbed her coat, petted JJ, and told him she would see him in a bit.

They walked out the door. David was respectful. He held her hand as they came down the steps, so she wouldn't fall, and when they arrived at the car, he opened the door for her. As he stepped in and closed his door, he looked at her, smiled, and said, "You look beautiful tonight, Mary."

"Thank you." She returned the smile.

As they drove out of the driveway, David had the heated seats turned on low. They felt amazing. Mary tried her best to enjoy every season the Lord gave her, but winter was not her favorite. She didn't like the cold weather.

They arrived at the restaurant. He opened the door for her, and they walked inside. He pulled Mary's chair out for her, and as she sat down, she looked over to see her friend Patricia and her husband, Paul. They were out celebrating his new job. Patricia was dressed in an adorable outfit and always made any room she was in more beautiful.

Mary had mentioned to Patricia about David, but they had never met. Neither of them had known they would be having dinner at the same restaurant that evening.

The waiter came over and welcomed them as he handed David the wine menu. "Would you two like a glass of wine this evening?"

Mary looked at David and said, "Yes, I will have a glass, please." She was still overjoyed about her cottage. She almost felt a little overwhelmed. They both ordered glasses of cabernet and continued to look over the dinner menu.

The menu was filled with entrées that seemed irresistible. Deciding on one item was tough. David smiled at Mary as if he had made his final decision.

"What did you decide on, David?" Mary asked. She giggled and said, "I can't decide. I keep going back to the dessert menu."

The waiter returned to the table with their glasses of wine and asked if they were ready to order. Mary looked over at David, and he proceeded to place his order. Mary smiled and said to the waiter, "I will have the same entrée he ordered." David looked at her with surprise. She looked at him and said, "What? That's exactly what I was going to choose."

They toasted with a sip of their wine and then got up to say hello to Patricia and Paul, who both stood up and gave Mary a friendly hug.

"It's so nice to see you both here tonight. What a surprise." Mary introduced David to them. "Patricia and Paul, meet my friend David."

The conversation was pleasant. As Mary and David were getting ready to walk back over to their table, Patricia looked at Mary with a smirk as if to say, "Oh, he's handsome." Mary smiled and continued back to the table.

While they were waiting for their dinner to be served, David asked Mary how she was feeling about her manuscript being complete. She was a little anxious and happy that the book was done. She told him she had received an email from the publisher telling her it was about to go to first print. She wanted more than anything for it to be a bestseller, but most importantly, she hoped God would allow it to reach others as He spoke to their hearts.

David said, "Mary, I am very proud of you."

She told him her desire to be an author and write a book had always been in her heart. She couldn't thank God enough for the opportunity to see a dream become a reality finally. "The publisher told me I would be very happy, as the orders from retailers were amazing." Mary said she was still waiting for an email and had become anxious. She smiled and said, "I'm constantly asking God to give me peace." David smiled.

The conversation was healthy and meaningful. She proceeded to ask David about his life. "What are you up to these days?"

He started talking about his uncertainty about where his life was going. "After the divorce, I feel a little unsettled. I never wanted our marriage to end, but I've since realized I wasn't the leader I needed to be. I spent most of my focus on work, believing that providing was my priority and forgetting that the most important part of my role was to nurture, guide, and protect Pam in the Word of God. This has been a struggle for me. I have prayed for forgiveness, and I have prayed that one day Pam will forgive me."

David told Mary that Pam was a sweet girl. She loved David but could not handle their lifestyle any longer. He was sure that her watching him chase the things of the world rather than God had been difficult for her. "She prayed consistently for me, but I never changed," David said. "We didn't have any children, and as much as I wanted them, I am grateful for that."

Mary proceeded to share about her marriage to Edward and how she had developed trust issues and built walls around her heart. She wouldn't allow anyone to get close to her. Deep down in her heart, she thought she had forgiven him and had tried to forget the pain for years. However, with every new relationship, she felt guarded. She knew she was still carrying unforgiveness in her heart and continued to pray that God would help her.

David wanted to be honest with Mary and told her about the affair he had had while married to Pam. "She was an honest woman and a great wife. She was always there for me and tried hard to share her concerns with me. I wouldn't listen. I didn't want to hear the truth. My pride got the best of me. It's too late now for Pam and me, but I would like to think I have learned my lesson."

Mary at once felt Pam's pain. She no longer looked at David the same way. She realized she was judging him. She began to pray to herself. *Father, help me to be his friend. Please don't allow me to judge David, as he is seeking to be honest with me and obviously has pain and regret in his life for what he did. Father, we all need to be dependent on you every day. Why do we think we can do this on our own?*

Dinner was fantastic, as usual, and the conversation was enjoyable. When the waiter returned to clear their dinner dishes, he asked if they were ready for dessert. Mary knew she didn't have room for anything else and made a funny comment to David. "I should have had dessert first," she said with a smirk.

As they got up to leave, he looked at her and said, "Mary, thank you for a great evening."

He drove her home and walked her to the door, and they said good night.

8

WINTER HAS ARRIVED

The time had come for Mary to embrace the first winter storm of the year. She spent most of the day covering outside water faucets so they wouldn't freeze and putting lawn furniture away. The storm was predicted to drop about six inches of snow after midnight. It was close to bedtime, and she was tired from a hard day of work. She had missed her writing that day but decided she would have more time tomorrow. She turned on the television to find a quick show to watch and flipped through the channels, but nothing interesting was on. She wondered what had happened to the wholesome shows she used to watch as a kid. Mary quickly turned off the TV and picked up a book from the coffee table.

Mary read for a while and began to drift off to sleep. She got up, flipped off the lights, and crawled into bed. JJ came right behind her.

The morning came quickly. Mary remembered the prediction of snow, so she jumped out of bed and went quickly to the window. The snow was still falling. There were about three inches already on the ground. It was beautiful. The ocean waves were crashing onto the shore. The sound of the ocean never got old to her.

The snow reminded her of days as a child sledding with her sisters and friends in the neighborhood. The amazing energy they'd had as kids had been almost never-ending. They would walk for fifteen minutes up tall hills to sled down time and time again for hours. Mary remembers how much fun it had been. Her mom had always made snow cream, and it was always delicious. Those were great memories for Mary, memories she never wanted to forget. She could still see the excitement on her mom's face when she heard the forecast of snow.

With excitement, Mary said, "JJ, it snowed last night. Mom will have to clear you a path to go potty." She threw on her sweats and tennis shoes, grabbed her jacket, turned on the coffeepot, and grabbed her snow shovel, which was resting by the steps just outside the back door. As she opened the door, the snow was blowing. She quickly cleared the steps and a path for JJ.

Mary walked back in, put JJ's sweater on, and said, "Let's go, buddy." With his tail wagging, he followed her back outside. JJ loved the snow too. He wanted to play awhile, but Mary was freezing. "Let's go back inside, JJ, and warm up a bit. We will come back later. I promise."

Her coffee had brewed, and she was happy. Mary loved coffee. She grabbed a mug, poured her coffee, and put some food out for JJ. She sat down in her chair by the window. After JJ finished eating, he jumped into her lap. They both stared out the window and watched the birds on the feeders. *Life is great*, she thought.

Suddenly, Mary heard a cry and scratches at the door. She quickly realized it was a kitten. "Oh goodness!" she exclaimed. "JJ, it's a tiny black kitten. It's freezing." She grabbed a blanket, picked the kitten up, quickly warmed some milk, and found a box to put the kitten in. She dropped the blanket in the box. The kitten was shivering. "You're a girl," Mary said. "I will name you Sunshine." Sunshine drank the warm milk, cuddled in her blanket, and fell asleep. Mary thanked Jesus for bringing the kitten to her, as Jesus knew she would take care of it. JJ was a little jealous, but that would soon pass. Sunshine had found a new home.

The phone rang. It was David. "Mary, are you OK? We have a lot of snow, huh?"

"Yes, David, thank you! I'm sitting here with JJ, drinking my coffee. I shoveled a path for him this morning, and you will never believe what happened next! Jesus brought a tiny black kitten to my door. She was so cold! I heated her warm milk, and she lapped it up. I have named her Sunshine," she said with a giggle. "She is now warm and sleeping snugly."

He was excited and happy for Mary. He knew Jesus had sent the kitten there for Mary to love. David shared with Mary that he was shoveling driveways for some of the widows in his neighborhood.

Mary replied, "That's so sweet, David. Please be careful. Thanks for checking on me." They said goodbye and hung up.

Mary sat in her chair and opened her Bible to read for a while when she heard the kitten stirring. She walked over to her box to peek and saw Sunshine looking up at her. Sunshine had the biggest, brightest brown eyes Mary had ever seen. She looked happy. Mary's heart smiled. She realized she didn't have any food for her but then remembered a can of tuna in water in the pantry. She opened the can and put some tuna down for her. "This will have to work until we can get out to the store." As Sunshine gobbled it up, she looked happy with the choice.

Mary had an old litter box from another cat she'd had. His name had been Bandit. He'd died a few years back. She missed him. She set up her litter box and placed it by the back door, on the tile floor. After Sunshine ate her tuna, Mary introduced her to her new place to go potty. Sunshine scratched around a bit, circled, and squatted. JJ ran over with curiosity. "JJ, Sunshine just used her litter box," Mary said with a giggle. "OK, girly, you should snuggle in your box and sleep for a while." Sunshine was so tiny. JJ was happy she was back in her box, as he still wasn't sure he wanted to share his mama. "JJ, you will be fine, baby. Come up here with me."

Mary sat back down in her chair and began reading her Bible. Mary had prayed for years that if God wanted her to be married again, He would send her a godly man. She wanted someone to share her life with but someone she knew was sincere about his walk with the Lord—someone who didn't just talk about Jesus but who had a strong desire to be like Him. She thought of David again and wondered if maybe he was the one. Jesus would let her know, she believed.

The phone rang. It was Victoria.

"Hi, Victoria. How are you? Are you snowed in too?"

"I am, but isn't the snow beautiful?"

Mary agreed. "I haven't seen you since our celebration dinner. What have you been up to?"

Victoria told her about a possible move to Charlotte, North Carolina. Her husband, John, had a new job that was too far for a commute, and he didn't want to travel every week to work, only spending the weekends at home.

"Oh, Victoria, Charlotte is more than three hours from here. How do you feel about moving? We will miss you so much if you move. When will you know for sure?"

"Well, that's another reason why I'm calling. We are going to Charlotte this coming Friday to look at a few houses. I wanted to ask if you could stop by to pick up my mail every day for me."

"Of course, Victoria. I wouldn't mind doing that at all. The snow should begin melting this afternoon, and I am going to try to get out to pick up—oh, I didn't tell you. Victoria, I have a new friend." She proceeded to tell her the story about Sunshine. "She's so adorable. JJ is still not sure he wants her around, but he should be OK."

"Mary, that's wonderful! You are right; Jesus did send you a new kitten. He knew you would love it forever."

"Thank you, Victoria. I need to go out later to get some cat food and more litter if the snow melts a little. If not, she will be fine until tomorrow. It's so great to hear from you, Victoria. Please know I will be praying for you and John to make the right decision about your move, and I will pick up your mail this weekend. Have a safe trip. I love you!"

"Love you back, Mary!"

As the morning sun brightened, the temperatures began to rise. The snow had stopped falling. It was still cold, but the snow was beginning to melt. Snow in South Carolina only happened occasionally, and it never stayed around long. This snowfall had been a welcome surprise.

Mary and JJ decided to walk down by the ocean. The seashells were steadily coming in with the waves. JJ was happy. He loved their walks on the beach. The smell and sound of the ocean were always a great reminder of the power of God for Mary. She was reminded of Genesis

1:10: "And God called the dry land Earth, and the gathering together of the waters called the Seas: and God saw that it was good." She loved that scripture.

The rest of the day was filled with chores and a couple of hours of writing. Before she knew it, the day had almost passed.

9

A CALL TO ENCOURAGE AND A SURPRISE DATE

Thursday morning, just before the sun began to shine, Mary heard a noise coming from the living room. It was a sound she hadn't heard before. As she got up to see where it was coming from, she was reminded of Sunshine. She had left her in the box just before bed to sleep. She heard the soft sounds of a meow and scratching on the box. Sunshine wanted out. Mary picked her up and set her down. She ran straight to her litter box, spun around, and squatted. Mary was delighted to see how easily she was being trained to her litter box. "I guess it is time to let her play inside the house. After all, she is part of the family now."

Mary yawned and stretched with a smile. She thanked Jesus for another day and asked the Holy Spirit to lead her. The temperatures were still in the forties, and there was still a little snow on the ground. She was sure it would all be melted by the afternoon.

Before her first drink of coffee, the phone rang. It was David. "Mary, good morning. Did you get a good night's rest?"

"I did, David. How about you?"

"I tossed and turned most of the night. Couldn't quit thinking about you."

"Well, I hope your thoughts were good."

"Ha ha, yes, they were. I know it's early, but I couldn't wait any longer. You don't have to tell me now, but I wanted to ask you out for a date tomorrow night."

"Oh," Mary said with hesitation. "What do you have in mind?"

"It will be a surprise."

"Well, I guess I can't pass up a surprise."

"Great. I will pick you up at six. Is that OK?"

"Yes, sounds great!"

Mary couldn't quit thinking about her call with David. Questions continued to run through her head. *Wonder what the surprise is. Where is he taking me? Why couldn't he sleep thinking about me?* As those thoughts continued, she began to pray. "Father, please give me peace. Remove this anxiety from me as I trust and follow you. Protect me, Father. In Jesus's name, amen."

As Mary was reading her Bible and praying, she glanced over to see JJ and Sunshine sleeping beside each other. JJ was happy to have another friend.

Mary got up to stretch and take a break when she looked down at her phone and saw that she had missed a call. She didn't recognize the number but saw she had a voicemail. She listened: "Hi, Mary. It's Tiffany. I met you at the grocery store the other day, and you left me your number. I wanted to say thank you for encouraging me. I guess you could tell I needed it. I was wondering if we could get together for lunch one day soon, as I would like to talk to you a little more. Maybe you can give me some advice. I hope to hear from you soon."

Mary was encouraged that Tiffany had called and knew she needed to make time for her soon. Lunch would be awesome with Tiffany, she thought. The Lord had given Mary a heart for young girls, as she knew they needed someone to share the truth with them in love. She never wanted anyone to go through the heartbreak she had gone through at such a young age. If she could help someone, she wanted to. She quickly hit redial and called Tiffany back.

When the young girl answered the phone, Mary said, "Hi, Tiffany. It's Mary. Are you working today? I would love to meet you for lunch if you have the time."

Tiffany was excited to hear from her and agreed to lunch at noon. She asked if the Mexican restaurant on Patterson Avenue was an acceptable choice.

"Sounds great. I'll see you in just a little while. Can't wait to see you, Tiffany," Mary said.

After they hung up, Mary began to pray. "Father, help me to be a friend to Tiffany. There are so many who need encouragement and the truth. Thank you for the heart you have given me for others. May I always be available as you lead me. Give me the words to say, as you know her needs. In your Word, in Luke 12:12, you tell us, 'For the Holy Spirit will teach you at that time what you should say.' Thank you for leading me. In Jesus's name, amen."

She spent her morning catching up on work that needed to be done. Her days off Mr. Henry had given her were coming to an end. Monday was another workday. She missed her job but enjoyed every second she had off. God knew she needed this time, and Mr. Henry knew it too.

At 11:45, Mary got in her car to meet Tiffany for lunch. As she arrived at the restaurant, she saw Tiffany sitting in her car. *She must be waiting for me*, Mary thought. Tiffany was about five foot five. She had strawberry-blonde hair and a beautiful smile. Mary walked over to her car and said, "Hi, Tiffany. Let's go inside and get some lunch. I'm hungry." They both laughed and walked inside. Mary had a way of making everyone feel at ease. She genuinely loved from her heart, and it was obvious.

They sat down in a corner booth, and the waiter came over to get their drink orders.

Mary remembered the delicious tacos the girls had brought over when they delivered the boxes to her apartment, so that was what she ordered. Tiffany ordered a couple of tacos and a drink. Mary could tell she was a little uncomfortable, and she understood that. After all, she didn't know her at all. As the waiter came over and brought their drinks, Mary asked her if she was OK.

Tiffany began to tell her why she had been upset. "Mary, I'm so scared.

My boyfriend, James, is trying to push me into having sex with him, and I don't feel right about it. I love him, and I am afraid he will leave me if I don't. The girls in my class talk about sex all the time like it's nothing, but I don't feel that way. I feel like I don't fit in, and that is a terrible feeling. Peer pressure is so real. I'm just having a hard time navigating all of this."

Mary quickly said, "Tiffany, don't!"

Tiffany looked surprised at how quickly Mary responded, but Mary had been there already and had made the wrong choice.

Mary went on to say how proud she was of Tiffany for reaching out to her before making an emotional decision. "I promise you it will affect your life forever." Mary told her the story of having the same emotions and following through with a choice of temptation. It was a choice she would always regret, and she told Tiffany what a negative impact it had on her life emotionally.

Tiffany was fearful that her boyfriend would break up with her, and Mary told her that if he did, he didn't love or respect her or that she was making the best decision for herself. Mary said, "Tiffany, maybe you should talk with James and tell him that you have no desire to have sex with him and that your heart will not allow it. Be honest with him. Don't allow him to intimidate you in any way. I can tell your heart is right before God, or we wouldn't be having this conversation. Thank you for reaching out to me. You understand that He is nudging you to make the right decision, don't you? Follow Him, girl. You will never regret it!

"Maybe after you talk to him, give him this scripture. Maybe your witness will help him to make the right decisions for himself and others in the future. First Corinthians 6:18–20 says, 'Flee from sexual immorality. All other sins a person commits are outside the body, but whoever sins sexually sins against their own body. Do you not know that your bodies are temples of the Holy Spirit, who is in you, whom you have received from God? You are not your own; you were bought at a price. Therefore, honor God with your bodies.'"

Mary at once saw Tiffany's countenance change. Tiffany looked at Mary with joy and realized the love of Jesus and how His conviction had protected her. She was grateful that Mary followed His leadership to minister to her.

Their food was delivered to the table, and Mary asked if she could pray. Tiffany agreed with a look of gratefulness. They held hands, and Mary began to pray. "Father, thank you for my new friend, Tiffany. Thank you for leading us daily and allowing us to see your will for our lives. Father, we know peer pressure is real, and I am grateful for Tiffany's heart that she didn't choose to follow that path. Yes, sometimes we feel left out in this world, as so many are lost and are being led astray. Please help my new friend stay strong in her faith to continue to follow you all the days of her life. We know you will bless her. Continue to give her great discernment as she navigates through this dark world, and may she continue to be the light that shines in the darkness. Bless those, Father, who didn't make the right choice with their bodies. Redirect them to the cross as you forgive them and heal their hearts. Use this food to nourish us, Father. In Jesus's name, amen."

The atmosphere at the table had changed. Mary felt joy from Tiffany and knew exactly where it was coming from. God had protected her, and she was grateful.

As they finished their lunch, Mary told Tiffany to call anytime. "I will always be here for you. I promise!" Mary paid the bill, and they walked out to their cars. She hugged Tiffany and told her how proud of her she was. "Call me anytime, Tiffany."

She handed Tiffany a piece of paper and asked her to keep it with her always. Proverbs 4:23 was written on it: "Above all else, guard your heart, for everything you do flows from it."

"Tiffany," Mary said, "I didn't protect my heart well when I was your age. Always follow Jesus's guidance. He will protect you."

When Mary got back home, she took JJ for a walk on the beach. It was chilly, but she didn't care. She found peace there. Something drew her to the ocean, and she went for walks as often as she could.

Another day came to an end. After reading for a while with Sunshine and JJ lying by her, she turned off the light, prayed, and drifted off to sleep.

As the sun shone through the window in her bedroom, Mary got out of bed and opened the blinds to see the world outside, waking up. The sound of the ocean waves never got old. *It looks like it's going to be a beautiful day.* Sunshine had been prowling around the cottage most of the night but found her way back to bed. She was lying close to JJ. They both began to stretch. "OK, boy, let's get you outside." Mary turned her coffeepot on, grabbed her jacket, and went for a quick walk.

Mary decided that morning that she wanted a quiche. She poured her coffee and pulled everything she needed out of the refrigerator. She turned the oven on to preheat and began preparing her quiche.

It was Friday, and it was going to be a special day; she looked forward to her surprise date with David. Mary was loving her time off from work. She knew it was coming to an end quickly but was still grateful for the time off.

She stood in her closet with no idea what to wear. *Surprise*, she thought. *Where are we going? Are we going to dinner?* She pulled a beautiful navy blue dress off the rack and a silk scarf. *I think this will work for almost anything. My navy heels will look great with this dress as well. There you go! This will work great.* Mary remembered buying the dress. She and Patricia had gone shopping one afternoon at the Galleria. They'd had a great time together that day.

She thought *I hadn't seen Patricia since my last date with David when we saw her and Paul at the restaurant. Maybe I will call her, and we can talk while I'm doing my makeup and hair.* She picked up the phone and called her.

Patricia answered. "Mary, hi! I haven't talked to you in a while. How are you?"

"Busy, as always, you know. I must go back to work on Monday. I'm looking forward to it, and I've really missed Mr. Henry. We have so much to catch up on. I was just thinking about you. I am going on another date with David tonight, and I'm wearing the navy blue dress I bought when we were shopping at the Galleria a few weeks ago. Do you remember the one?"

Patricia answered, "Yes, I do. You will look adorable. Where are you two going?"

"I wish I knew. I guess it's a surprise. That was what David said anyway."

"Ha ha, that will be fun!"

"I hope so, Patricia. Hey, did I tell you about Sunshine?"

"Sunshine? No, tell me."

Mary proceeded to tell the story of how the new kitten had found her home.

"Oh, Mary, that's just great! I am sure Sunshine will have many great years with you and JJ. Who knows? Maybe David will also be in your future."

Mary's heart started pounding. "Oh no! I can't imagine that. I love my life just like it is, Patricia."

"I know, Mary, but you never know, right?"

"I guess." Mary also told Patricia about her new friend Tiffany and their lunch that day, and she asked Patricia to continue to pray for her. "Patricia, I'd better get going. David should be here soon." They hung up, and for some reason, Mary had lost some excitement about her date. The thought of being married again was too much for her to imagine.

Mary finished her makeup and hair and was ready for her date. She quickly fed JJ and Sunshine and slipped on her other shoes to take JJ out for a walk.

As soon as they were back inside, a car pulled into the driveway. It was David. He had a gift box of chocolates in his hand. The box looked expensive. She knew the brand and had always wanted to try it, as she loved great chocolate but could never afford it.

"David, it's so good to see you," she said, and he handed her the chocolate. "Thank you so much. You are too much! You look handsome, David."

"Thank you, Mary. You look stunning."

She laid her chocolate on the counter and giggled. "I can't wait to try this!" She told JJ and Sunshine goodbye as they walked out the door.

David always seemed to be a gentleman. They both got in his car, and he started the engine. As he backed out of the driveway, Mary said with a smile, "So where are we going?"

"I can't tell you just yet."

"What? Why?" she said with a giggle.

They arrived at the airport. Mary was puzzled and concerned. "Why are we at the airport?"

"Well, I guess I must tell you now, mustn't I?"

"I guess you must," she said with a laugh.

"Mary, I have arranged a private flight for us this evening. Dinner in New York City at a restaurant highly suggested by a friend. Is that OK?"

"Well, of course. You really know how to surprise a girl, David."

He parked the car by the plane. A gentleman walked out and said, "Welcome aboard."

Sitting on a table in front of their seats were a bottle of champagne and two crystal glasses. "May I?" David said to her.

"Well, of course. What are we celebrating?"

"Mary, do you remember you just bought your first home?"

"Yes, of course I do."

"I am very proud of you—that's all."

She looked over at him with a tear going down her cheek. Mary didn't like a lot of attention and certainly didn't feel worthy of this kind of attention. They toasted with their first sip of champagne, and both smiled at each other. Mary felt butterflies in her stomach as she longed for love. She had never thought she would have that feeling again, until now.

The pilot announced the descent for landing, and the seat belt sign came on. They both stopped and connected their seat belts. Mary felt a little overwhelmed. She had never been on a private plane, let alone on a date. The plane landed safely and came to a stop. As they exited the plane, a gentleman in a tuxedo was standing next to a limousine. He opened the door for them to enter. David and Mary climbed in. He closed the door behind them. As they drove off, the driver confirmed the address of the restaurant to David. He agreed.

Mary said a silent prayer. *Father, continue to remind me that the things of this world mean nothing without you first in my life. Please don't allow me to get caught up in an imaginary world. I thank you for always guiding me. In Jesus's name, I pray. Amen.*

David looked over at Mary and asked if she was OK.

"Yes, I am, David. I was talking to the Lord," she said with a smile.

The driver parked in front of the restaurant and opened the door for them to exit the limousine.

David took Mary's hand, and they walked in together. The host came over and seated them in a candlelit corner booth. The waiter brought over the wine menu and asked if they wanted to order a bottle or a glass. Mary looked at David and the waiter and said, "Thank you, but I will have water with lemon, please." David seemed a little disappointed that she wasn't having any wine. She smiled at him and said, "We just had champagne."

David didn't know Mary well. He knew she loved Jesus but didn't know how disciplined she was. He asked Mary if she minded if he had a glass.

She said, "Of course not, David." He then ordered a glass of cabernet.

As they looked over the menu, she was having a hard time deciding what she wanted.

The music caught her attention. A jazz band was playing in the background. She loved jazz music. When the waiter came back over to bring David's glass of wine, Mary looked over at David with a smile to reassure him she was not judging him. They both ordered their dinner choices. After the waiter left the table, David got up, walked over to Mary, and asked if he could have this dance. There was a space not far from the table where they could dance without bumping into anything. He led her there, and they began to dance. It was an amazing feeling for Mary, as she had been lonely for so long for a companion she could feel this way with.

It felt like a perfect night. As the song ended, David led her back to their table. Mary told David, "Thank you for such an amazing evening. You really know how to treat a girl, don't you?"

David smiled back at her and said, "Thank you, Mary, for coming with me. I was afraid you would ask me to take you back home when we pulled up at the airport."

"Ha ha," Mary said. "Surprised you, didn't I?"

The waiter brought their salads and added fresh parmesan cheese and cracked black pepper. The salad had crispy onions and homemade croutons on top. It looked yummy, and they were both hungry. David didn't offer to say the blessing, so Mary asked David if he minded if she thanked the Lord for their food.

With a humble but embarrassed look, David said, "Of course, Mary."

Mary began to pray. "Father, thank you for this evening with David. Thank you for the food you have supplied us. I pray, Father, that you bless it and bless us. Use this food and company to nourish our bodies. May we always be reminded that everything you give is a gift. In Jesus's name, we pray. Amen."

The conversation between David and Mary was always enjoyable until she started talking about her faith and Jesus. He always seemed to be a little uncomfortable, so Mary asked him if he attended church anywhere. His answer—no—didn't surprise Mary. Mary asked him if he just hadn't found a church he was comfortable with.

"It just feels like a big celebration or something to me," he said.

Mary understood that feeling. She hadn't found a church she really enjoyed either. She asked, "David, do you go to any home churches or men's meetings?"

"No," David said. "I need to be more proactive in seeking a place for sure. It's just that all my life, I've struggled with religion. I pray, Mary, and I know Jesus died for my sins. I just haven't felt like I really fit in anywhere. Something feels very strange to me. Jesus is love, and so many times, I feel judged."

Mary told David that she had grown up in church and attending church had been important to her as a child, but she had never been taught the gospel in the way she knew it now. She knew the presence of the Holy Spirit, and she had chased that feeling her entire life. The world had become a mess. There was so much division. The right was left. Left was right. "Only God can help us," she said, and he agreed. Mary then said, "I can tell you this: over time, life's lessons have helped me. Without my faith and my relationship with Jesus, I can't imagine how I would have ever gotten through so far. He is my strength, David."

Mary thought that Jesus was leading more Christians to stand up for the true gospel and that many were beginning to have more fellowship and church in their private homes. David agreed and thought that was a great idea.

Mary enjoyed sharing her heart about Jesus. "People need to be able to fellowship with other believers and enjoy their time together without feeling judged. We are all in need of Jesus, and we need to pray for one another and understand that without Him as the center of our lives, we will not find joy and peace in our hearts. Not as He gives it anyway. True joy and peace only come from Him! Everything else is deception, and it's easy to get caught up in the lie of the Enemy. When we make Jesus the center of our lives, we can believe that we will see the glory of God!"

Mary prayed for David that he would come to know God's love for him regardless of his concerns and that his heart would be drawn closer to the Lord. She truly understood his concerns and wanted to be a friend—not to judge him but to listen and encourage him.

The waiter came by to bring their entrées.

"Yummy," Mary said. "This looks delicious." David smiled in agreement.

Their conversation continued to go well, and they had a wonderful time together.

The waiter then brought over a dessert tray.

Mary said, "Oh my goodness. How do you pick one? I am stuffed. The meal was delicious."

David told the waiter he would have the chocolate brownie with chocolate syrup and ice cream. "Also, could you bring two spoons, please?"

Mary laughed. "OK, I will try just one bite."

In about five minutes, the waiter brought their dessert, and they finished every bite.

"That was so yummy," said Mary. "I couldn't eat anything else if I wanted to."

David laughed and replied, "Me either. I ate way too much!"

Mary thanked David again for a great evening.

"It was my pleasure, Mary." David paid the waiter for dinner and texted his driver to pick them up. They got up to leave, and as David reached for her hand, they left the restaurant.

Mary prayed, *Lord, thank you for a beautiful, relaxing night. Guide me and protect me. May your will be done in my life.*

The driver was already waiting outside. He opened the door of the limousine to let them in, and they headed back to the airport. The flight was restful and lovely. The conversation was good, and they both were a little tired. It seemed like minutes before the pilot came on to say they were landing. When the seat belt light came on, they both fastened their seat belts, and Mary prayed for a safe landing. All was well, and they were back on the ground.

David's car was parked close, so there wasn't a long walk. He opened the door and smiled, and Mary climbed in. It had been a relaxing evening. David thanked Mary again. The drive back to the cottage was peaceful.

As much as she'd enjoyed her time with David that night, she knew she would take it slowly. She couldn't take another heartbreak.

Before going to bed, Mary checked her email. She quickly saw an email from Johnathon. It read,

Mary, the first printing of your book is complete. Retailers all over the world have chosen to buy, and a few have inquired about you doing book signings. I know you are busy with your job but wanted to discuss some days next month when you may be available. The shipment you requested was sent out a few days ago and should arrive at your place today. Let's set a time for a call in a few days so we can go over those dates and the retail sales. Let me know a time that works best for you. Congratulations, Mary! Prepare for an amazing journey.

Johnathon

It was Friday, and her package should have arrived. She hadn't seen a box when she came in. *Maybe it's at the back door*, she thought. She got up and ran to the door, and there it was. "Wow! Oh, my goodness! My books are here, JJ. I am so happy I checked my email." He heard her and ran to her in excitement. She picked the box up and brought it inside. She couldn't get it open quickly enough, as she could not wait to see the book.

After she opened the box, she picked up one of her books and began to cry. "Seriously, Lord, thank you so much! It's beautiful. It's perfect. It's a dream come true. Lord, you are so good to me. Lord, I give you all the glory!"

Mary realized God was using her testimony to reach others. She wanted to stay humble in the understanding that only because of Him could she write the words in her book. Her life had not been perfect, and her desire was to prayerfully help others in some small way. She also knew that God had written her story, and nothing she endured was a surprise to Him.

10

SPRING IS IN THE AIR

Mary woke up to the sound of birds singing. *How beautiful*, she thought, thanking Jesus for the birds. The thought of spring made her happy. Spring and fall were her favorite seasons. She got out of bed, opened the blinds, watched the ocean waves come onto the shore, and thought about a long walk on the beach with her coffee. JJ was still lying on the bed, and as she glanced back over at him, she smiled. Sunshine dashed from under the bed and ran into the other room. "You guys make me happy. Do you know that?" They brought her a lot of joy, and they were now all settled in their new home. God had given her two great gifts in JJ and Sunshine. Mary was happy and recognized them as true gifts from heaven.

She remembered her book and ran into the living room, where the box sat. She picked up her book again and flipped through it. She was sure she had just had an amazing dream and had to pinch herself as she held it in her hands. She then decided she would take her coffee on the beach and spend time with the Lord.

She threw on sweats and tennis shoes, brushed her teeth, and combed her hair. The temperatures were still brisk. She grabbed her coffee as well as her jacket and began walking to the sand. Mary loved the mornings.

She especially loved them when the weather was clear, and she could walk out on the beach.

As she started walking, she saw the perfect seashell. It was worn but had a special look. It had many broken edges, but they had been smoothed out over time. It reminded Mary of her life and how God was healing it. He was making all things new. "This one is a keeper," she said. She stopped, looked over toward her cottage, and again thanked Jesus for her new book, which sat in a box inside. She began to cry, realizing God was using her heart to reach others. That brought Mary to a place of contentment in her heart.

Mary began to pray. "Lord, you never cease to amaze me. Thank you for my new life. In all my mistakes in life, you have never left me. You have always loved me, and you always forgive me. Thank you for carrying me through life's storms and always showing me the way. Even when I chose my own path, you redirected me and always reassured me of your love for me. Lord, I am reminded of your Word today in Romans 8:28: 'And we know that all things God works for the good of those who love him, who have been called according to his purpose.' I am humbled, Lord, that you call me by my name. It still overwhelms me that you call me your friend. May I never have doubt but always know the fullness of your love, power, goodness, peace, and joy and everything you are as I seek to be more like you. Help me to continue following you as you guide me, Father. In Jesus's name, I pray. Amen."

As Mary continued to walk along the beach, she saw someone walking toward her. *Hmm. That's a little odd, but I'm sure it's just a tourist getting away from his or her routine for a bit.* As the person got closer, she realized it was a man. He seemed to be enjoying his walk as she watched him stop to pick up a few shells. She thought of turning to go back but decided to keep walking.

As the guy walked closer, Mary could tell he looked relaxed and was enjoying his walk. She saw him bend down a few times as if picking up shells. She was walking on the edge of the water and saw a crab close to her foot. "Uh-oh," she said, running back to the shore, giggling. When she looked up, there he was.

"Are you OK?" He giggled too.

"Yes, I'm OK," she said, laughing. "I thought that crab was going to bite me."

"Ha ha," he said. "It didn't bite you, did it?"

"No, thank God."

"Great. Now, let's start over. Hi. My name is Michael."

"Hi, Michael. I'm Mary. Do you live here, Michael?"

"No. Not yet, anyway. I rented a house just a few houses down for the spring and summer. I'm an author. I'm starting a new book and wanted a peaceful place to hang out for a while."

"Well, you picked the perfect place for writing. I am an author, too. I just received copies of my first book in the mail yesterday."

"You're kidding me, aren't you?"

"No, I'm not kidding at all."

"That's so funny, isn't it? It's almost like we were supposed to run into each other, huh?" he said, and Mary laughed. "What do you like to write about, Mary?"

"Oh, I write a lot about real life and Jesus. What about you?"

"That is very interesting. Sounds like a great read. Well, I write a lot about life too. Mostly about how we all need each other to get through this life."

"That makes this a lot more interesting," Mary replied. "OK, Michael, now you have me interested in reading one of your books. Where can I buy it?"

"Are you kidding me? I have one with me. You can have one. I may even autograph it for you."

"Sounds like a deal," Mary said. "I have one for you too. Maybe I will autograph it for you as well."

"This is weird, isn't it?" Their conversation felt a little awkward.

"Yeah, I didn't plan on this today for sure," Mary said.

"Where do you live, Mary?"

"I live in a cottage just up the beach a bit." Mary was reluctant to tell Michael where she lived. After all, she'd just met him and had no real idea who he was or where he came from. "Let's meet back here in the morning, and we can exchange books, huh?"

Michael replied, "That sounds great! Same time?"

"Yes," Mary said. "Well, it was nice meeting you, Michael. I will see you in the morning." They smiled at each other and walked away in opposite directions.

When Mary arrived back at the cottage, her head was spinning with questions and thoughts. *What was that about, Lord?* She thanked Him for the introduction but was puzzled about what was going on. *One day at a time, sweet Jesus.* She could see Him smile back at her.

Mary spent the day trying to get everything organized for her return to work on Monday. She sat on the floor, played with JJ for a few minutes, and remembered she had not had breakfast. "It's time for me to have breakfast, buddy," she said. "My tummy is grumbling." She got up and walked to the kitchen. Trying to decide what she wanted, she thought a great bowl of oatmeal would be amazing. *Maybe I will add some granola and dried cranberries.* Mary tried hard to eat healthily and exercise every day. She hadn't always done well. It took a lot of discipline for her. Pasta and bread were still her favorite comfort foods.

Mary sat in her chair by the window and began to write. She had a lot of thoughts she needed to put down on paper. She wrote in her journal almost every day. This helped her to keep her thoughts in some order and helped her to make sense of things. She also shared about her time with the Lord and the ways He was working in her life. She loved to go back and read her journal occasionally to be reminded of how faithful God had been to her. Mary had grown tremendously in her faith. She spent a lot of time talking to Jesus. James 4:8 was one of her favorite scriptures: "Draw nigh to God, and he will draw nigh to you."

Mary realized she had a text and looked down to read it. It was from Karen. She was inviting Mary to lunch tomorrow to catch up and thought it would be a good idea if the girls all met if possible. Mary told her about her morning meeting with Michael. "It felt so awkward, Karen. We are meeting again in the morning at the same place to exchange books. He's an author, too. He's here for the spring and summer to finish his next book."

"Oh, Mary, that sounds wonderful. Hey, can you start a group text about lunch tomorrow? It may have to be a little later for me, around one."

They said goodbye, and Mary sent a group text: "Lunch tomorrow at the café, girls?"

They all agreed that one o'clock would be great. They had so much to talk about and catch up on. She was excited to tell her friends about her date with David and the surprise she'd had at the beach that morning.

Thoughts of Michael and what felt like a divine appointment stayed on her mind most of the day. Michael was attractive, and he had a peace about him that she was attracted to. It was refreshing, she thought. She realized she needed to get out one of her books to bring to him in the morning, so she reached into the box and grabbed one. She sat down to autograph it and thought she would add a few words. She wrote, "Michael, from one author to the next, I pray your days are filled with joy, and your heart is constantly reminded of how much Jesus loves you." She then signed it and closed the book.

The day went quickly, and Mary was excited about meeting Michael in the morning as well as the girls for lunch. She made herself dinner, fed JJ and Sunshine, and sat down with a hot cup of ginger tea. She was happy with her life. She loved having her home to herself, and her furry friends were great company for her. She enjoyed being by herself and didn't feel the need for a husband. For the first time in a lot of years, Mary felt secure in herself and found peace and strength in who mattered the most: her Father in heaven. She'd had no idea until now how far away from God she had been in the past. *Life truly is good*, she thought.

Mary began to pray. "Lord, thank you for being such an amazing Father. Thank you for the security I have found in you. You are my everything. Lord, I have prayed this before and will continue to ask: if I am ever to be married again, please bring me a godly man. I can't imagine marrying anyone else."

Mary grabbed her laptop to write for a while before bed. The cottage was quiet, and she needed to unwind from the day. Writing was always relaxing for her. As she opened her laptop, she had a thought that surprised her: *Will I ever be a mom?* Mary was still young, in her late twenties. She wanted kids, and she wanted a family, but she wanted to be sure she made the right choice, as she wanted to be in love and have the perfect marriage. She wanted to be the perfect mom. Mary at once said, "Lord, help me trust you and lean on you for the right decisions always."

After writing for about an hour, Mary closed her laptop and crawled into bed.

Before she knew it, the sun was coming up. She could feel JJ tucked beside her. She cuddled with him and said, "Buddy, it's already morning. We'd better get up and get going. I have a lot to get done today." She thought about having to meet Michael at the beach in about an hour.

She turned on her coffeepot. She knew coffee was a must. Mary was feeling rushed and realized she was getting a little nervous. Life was taking her to places she wasn't sure she was comfortable with. Although she really liked David and enjoyed being with him, she was confused as to why she had met Michael now.

Life can really get interesting, can't it? she said. She quickly brushed her hair, brushed her teeth, and threw on a pair of sweats, tennis shoes, and a little makeup. As she was walking out the door, she realized she had not grabbed her book, so she went back inside to get it. She walked back out and began to pray. "Lord, help me to trust you. In Jesus's name, amen."

She talked to herself all the way to the shore to reassure herself that all was going to be OK. *Michael could be a good friend,* she thought. She didn't see him at first and continued to walk while looking down at the seashells washing onto the shore when, at once, she saw a magnificent shell. *Wow,* she thought. *That is the most beautiful shell I have ever seen.* She reached down to pick it up. It was a large shell that looked as if it had traveled for years and been placed there just for her. It had broken over the years, but the tossing and turning from the sea had smoothed the edges into the shape of a perfect heart.

A tear fell from her eye as she realized God was speaking to her through this shell to say, "Mary, I love you!"

Mary felt immediate peace. "Thank you, Lord."

As she continued to walk, carrying her book, she saw Michael coming in her direction. He waved as if to say, "I see you, Mary." Finally, they met again. He was charming and smiled at her in a way Mary had never seen or felt. She almost felt as if she had already known him. She couldn't tell. He had a peaceful, confident smile, and it warmed her heart. It felt real, and she felt it in her heart. They both giggled as they exchanged books. Michael told Mary he had been up late last night, thinking about how they had met and how strange it was.

Mary agreed. "Yes, I certainly had no idea I would run into you yesterday while I was here. It's very nice to meet you, and I will read your book."

Mary told Michael she needed to get back home, as she had lunch with friends that day. He gave her the same smile, and it warmed her heart again. He said, "I guess I will spend the afternoon reading instead of writing. I am excited about reading your new book, Mary. I see the reviews are outstanding already, and it was just released. That is so exciting!"

With a humble smile, Mary said, "Thank you, Michael. I hope to spend some time later today reading yours too. Being a new author is very exciting, isn't it?"

Michael asked Mary when she wanted to meet again.

"How about next week? Saturday morning at nine? I have been off work for almost two weeks, moving and everything. My boss was kind to give me the time off. But the time is coming to an end soon, and I must go back to work on Monday." As they turned to walk away, Mary was excited. She wasn't sure why. She almost felt as if she were meeting him in secret or something, and the entire situation felt like a mystery. After all, he was an author, too.

She hurried back home, realizing she hadn't fed JJ and Sunshine, and she was getting a little hungry. They both greeted her at the door. She opened their food and bent down to put it in the bowls. She was slicing a piece of her homemade bread and putting it in the toaster when the phone rang. She looked down to see it was Patricia. Patricia asked Mary if she could borrow a scarf she loved and if Mary would bring it with her to lunch.

Mary said, "Of course you can. I will grab it now, so I don't forget."

Patricia said, "Thank you, and I can't wait to see you later." They were all excited about their lunch date. They had so much to catch up on.

11

GIRLS' LUNCH OUT

Mary drove to the restaurant to meet her friends for lunch. As she arrived at the restaurant, she saw Patricia walking inside. Mary parked and called for her to come over to get the scarf she wanted to borrow.

Patricia ran over and gave her a big hug. "Thank you so much. Mary, I've missed you."

"I know, Patricia; I have missed you too. Today will be great! I can't wait to catch up."

They walked into the restaurant together, and Victoria and Karen were already seated. As Mary and Patricia approached the table, Victoria and Karen stood up, and they exchanged hugs. Mary told the girls how happy she was that they were all together. "We should do this at least once a week. I have missed all of you so much."

The waiter then came over and got everyone's drink order. They all ordered water with lemon, and as they were ordering the water, Victoria looked over and said, "Should we?"

Mary knew exactly what she was asking. "Yes, one glass would be great."

Karen asked the waiter if they could get a wine menu. As the waiter left to get it, the girls giggled at one another. They felt a little bit silly having a glass of wine at lunch, but they knew they would share a lot of great conversations and had a need to celebrate.

The waiter brought the wine and lunch menus, and all agreed on the same chardonnay except Patricia. She ordered a glass of lemonade. As they glanced at the lunch menu, Patricia said, "Girls, let's get an appetizer we can share." They all agreed on the fried zucchini. They remembered how good it had been the last time they'd had it, and the dip that came with it was yummy. They all placed their orders and continued to enjoy one another.

The conversations at the table were fun. They all took turns talking about their latest life experiences. Victoria talked about John, their trip to Charlotte, and how her husband's job offer was going. They had not found a house but continued to look. His job didn't start until June, so they had a little more time.

Victoria didn't really want to move, but she knew she needed to support John, as he was the provider financially. She also knew the drive would not be that difficult to visit Mary, Karen, and Patricia as often as she could. They were all sad but agreed they could take a road trip together to visit her in Charlotte as well.

"We all want what is best for you, Victoria."

Karen talked about how great it was to have left her job to be a stay-at-home wife. She and her husband were still trying to get pregnant, and she hoped it would happen soon. They wanted children badly and prayed that God would bless their family.

Patricia talked about Paul's new job and how well it was going. She loved that he didn't have to travel as much and could spend more time with her. She hadn't worked since they got married, and she found herself doing repetitive things every day, such as cleaning and cooking. She loved to bake and made some of the best bread in the world. She told the girls some great news she had. She had been about to burst from not saying anything before then. She was excited to see their reactions. She leaned into the table and told them the news. "Guess what, girls! Paul and I are going to have a baby. I was thankful you had me watch JJ during the move because I thought I was pregnant then, but it wasn't confirmed."

They all got out of their chairs and went over to Patricia for a big hug, and the excitement in the room was uncontainable. Karen's heart felt as if it skipped a beat, and she was happy for Patricia.

They all picked up their glasses and said cheers for all the great news so far. Patricia said, "We need to start getting together more often. It will take hours today to catch up. We may have to move this party somewhere else. Ha ha. Or they will charge us rent for the space."

They all laughed. Mary told Patricia they couldn't wait to have her baby shower.

The waiter brought over the food but had forgotten to bring the appetizer. They had been so busy talking that they hadn't even thought about it. It was time to eat now, and they were all hungry. The wineglasses were almost empty at that point, but they all knew they needed to be disciplined. "One glass is enough anyway," Mary said.

As they ate, Mary began to share. She talked about Sunshine. "Patricia, you know about her, but I don't think I have told you, girls." She shared how Sunshine had come into her life during the snowstorm. She pulled out her phone and showed everyone pictures. They were all overjoyed about the excitement Mary had about her new kitten. She then told the story of her date with David and how he had taken her to the airport. Mary said, "Girls, I wasn't sure if I should ask him to take me back home, but it was so much fun! I have never in my life had anyone treat me to a private flight to New York City for dinner."

The girls were mesmerized by her story; it sounded like a fairy tale. Mary agreed and said, "But it really did happen. I can say it's a first for me for sure." She also told them about meeting Tiffany and her story. She asked them to pray that she continued to make good decisions and protect her heart above all else, as Jesus called them all to do. She talked about her new book and receiving the box she had ordered when she got home from her date with David.

"As a gift to three of my favorite people." She reached into her bag, pulled out three copies of her book, and handed one to each of her friends. She had autographed them with special messages inside. They all got up in excitement and hugged Mary.

"We are so proud of you. We can't wait to read it. "Wow, Mary," said Victoria. "This is very pretty. I love the cover." They all looked through it for a few minutes but decided to wait till later to read what Mary had written to them.

"Oh, girls, that's not all. The other morning, I was walking on the beach with my coffee and ran into a stranger. His name is Michael. I saw him walking toward me but thought he was just a tourist or something. I was embarrassed because as I was walking on the edge of the water, a crab was coming toward me, and I thought it was going to bite me." She giggled. "I ran back to the shore, and there he was. I almost ran into him. Girls, he's an author too. He's only here for the spring and summer to finish a book. It was amazing. We met again this morning and exchanged books. He said he was going to start reading mine today. I hope he loves it. And I guess I will start reading his maybe later tonight before bed. We are meeting again on Saturday next week. You know my vacation time is over now. I go back to work on Monday." Mary was excited but knew she would miss her time at home during the week. She had to stop to take a deep breath as she realized she'd just blurted out a lot in a short time. Feeling a little anxious, she finally stopped speaking.

Patricia asked why they were not meeting at the cottage.

Mary told her she wasn't comfortable telling him where she lived yet, so they were meeting on the beach. She giggled and said, "It feels a little mystical. I don't know. I kind of like it. I was going to turn around as I saw him getting closer, and I just couldn't." Mary was continuously trying to trust God more and be totally dependent on His leadership. She wanted to walk in the way in which He led her.

Karen leaned on the table and said, "Mary, what about David?"

"I know!" said Mary. "I don't seem to know anything anymore. I am asking the Lord to continue to help me trust Him and let Him lead as I follow."

They all knew Mary's desire to follow Jesus, and they also knew about the mistakes she had made many times by looking for love in all the wrong places.

Mary did not want to get ahead of the Lord ever again, because she knew He had the perfect plan for her life. "It's a lot of fun to follow Jesus, actually. You feel safe because you know that no one knows what's best for you more than He does," Mary said. "I've made a lot of mistakes by living on my own understanding. I don't want to do that ever again."

The girls finished their lunch and, as always, had a great time together. They had been at the restaurant for a couple of hours and realized they'd better get going. They all agreed they would make a point to get together soon and to stay in touch by text. Karen made Mary promise to send a group text to give them all updates about David and Michael. They all got up and left the restaurant.

12

BACK TO WORK

Mary fell asleep while reading Michael's book. She was up much later than she wanted, as she was having trouble putting it down. She was surprised at the similarities between their books. They shared the importance of having friends to walk through life with. She loved reading, and she was enjoying his book.

Mary woke up to the sound of her alarm going off. It startled her at first. It was 6:00 a.m. on Monday morning; the day for her to be back at work had come. She knew she would miss being at home but was excited about getting back into a routine. The forecast for the day seemed perfect, with temperatures in the high sixties and low seventies. As she lay there thinking about her day, she began to feel a little anxious.

She crawled out of bed and turned on her coffeepot. Sunshine was already up and stirring in the living room. She had a ball she loved playing with. It jingled as she patted it across the floor and chased it. Mary loved watching her play.

Mary wanted to take JJ for a walk on the beach, but she knew she would not have time that morning, and she also knew she would miss it. She sat down with her coffee, opened her Bible, and read Psalm 1:1–2: "Blessed is the one who does not walk in step with the wicked or stand in the way that sinners take or sit in the company of mockers, but whose delight is in the law of the Lord, and who meditates on his law day and night. That person is like a tree planted by streams of water, which yields its fruit in season and whose leaf does not wither—whatever they do prospers."

She began to pray. "Lord, your words are a light to my path. Thank you so much for teaching me your ways. I would be lost without you. Thank you for always correcting me when I'm wrong and helping me to see the truth. As I prepare for my time back at the office today, Lord, fill me with your presence and allow me to continue to grow to be more like you. Thank you, Lord, for healing my friend Mr. Henry for your glory. We will claim that today. I pray that he feels well and that filling in at my job did not put too much pressure on him. In Jesus's name, I pray. Amen."

Mary finished her reading and got into the shower. She had already laid out the clothes she wanted to wear. She started thinking about JJ and how he would be without her. She laughed and thought maybe they would both get some rest. *None of us had a lot of time to do that when I was off.* She was satisfied with how she'd spent her time, and being settled in her new cottage was a blessing.

After she was dressed, she poured herself another cup of coffee and decided to make a piece of toast. *Raspberry jelly sounds good this morning,* she thought. She ate quickly, grabbed her keys and purse, and locked the door behind her.

The drive to the inn was much faster, as the cottage was about fifteen minutes closer than her apartment. She loved that. She knew she would be able to come home for lunch and enjoy some time without feeling rushed to get back. As she drove up the long entrance, she felt peace. She loved the colors of the flowers and trees blooming. It was glorious, she thought.

As she walked in, Mr. Henry was standing there. He looked good. He didn't look as tired as he had the last time she'd seen him. He welcomed her back and told her he'd missed her. He followed her to her office and apologized for not getting over to see her new cottage, but he had been busier than he'd thought he would be.

The revenue at the hotel had picked up quite a bit since COVID had finally gone away. It was a welcome change because everything had been at a standstill for so long.

They went over the schedule for the week together, and he shared with her about last week's activities. They were happy about the schedule of events coming up and felt everything was clear for the week ahead.

She then looked over at Mr. Henry and told him how much she had missed him and had been praying for him. He said he knew she had been and thanked her.

"Tell me, Mr. Henry. How are your appointments going?"

He told her that the treatment was going well and that he felt better. He would have a few other tests at the end of the week, and that would give him a much better idea. Mary was anxious to hear the results. He then told Mary he would let her get back to work and walked out of her office. She smiled back at him and said, "I will keep praying that your body be healed, Mr. Henry."

He walked back over to her desk, patted her on the back, and said, "Thank you so much, Mary."

Mary quickly checked her personal email and saw an email from her publisher. The subject line read, "Update." She proceeded to open the email. It read,

> Congratulations, Mary, on the revenue from the sale of your book. Your second print has been shipped already, and your book has now become a *New York Times* bestseller. Everyone's talking about it.

She almost fell out of her chair. She surprised herself when she felt a little nervous, as this was a big deal. Her book had become popular, but she had no idea the revenue it had created. For Mary, it wasn't about that anyway.

Mary wanted more than anything for lives to be changed in Jesus's name. She began to pray. "Lord, I feel as if my life is getting ready to change dramatically, and I'm not sure I like it. Please give me peace. You know how I like knowing what's always going on, and I'm feeling a little uncertain right now. No matter what, Lord, I pray that my book glorifies you and that people come to know you in a personal way. I pray lives are changed for your glory! I trust that you will lead me and carry me to the end. In Jesus's name, I pray. Amen."

Mary picked up her phone to text the girls and give them the news, when she saw she had a text from David. He was congratulating her on her new book. *Wow,* she thought. *How does he know this already?* She replied, "Thank you, David. How did you know?"

His response made Mary uncomfortable: "Are you kidding me? All you need to do is open social media. Everyone's talking about it. It was very exciting for me to see! I can't believe I am very good friends with a famous author, Mary. Don't forget, I knew you before you were famous, haha."

Mary put the phone down in disbelief and prayed again. "Lord, what's going on with my book? I know you wanted it to be read by many, but I'm not sure I'm ready for this."

The Lord responded in a soft voice, "You are ready, Mary. Just stay with me."

She thought of Proverbs 21:31: "The horse is made ready for the day of battle, but victory rests with the Lord."

"Will this be a battle, Lord?" she said.

"No, Mary, it may feel like it at times, but I have prepared you. You will do well. Remember, your words are my words. Did I not tell you if you believe, you would see my glory?"

Mary knew she had to focus on her work, as she had barely gotten anything done, and it would soon be lunchtime. She spent the rest of the morning with new clients, and a couple of them were already aware of her book. They mentioned it to her and congratulated her. She wasn't sure she wanted all the attention she was getting from her book so quickly and felt a little out of her comfort zone. She was excited but began to fear the requirements of her time, as she was finally finding a balance. She didn't want to deviate from that. She was comforted by Isaiah 41:10: "So do not fear, for I am with you; do not be dismayed, for I am your God. I will strengthen you and help you; I will uphold you with my righteous right hand." God always seemed to encourage Mary through His Word. He knew she would be afraid, but He also knew she was prepared for the journey He had given her.

The morning went quickly, and it was time for her lunch break. She enjoyed going home for lunch, as it gave her time to spend with JJ and take him outside for a walk. Mary was a little overwhelmed and thought about how good a hamburger and french fries would be. On her way home, she drove through the drive-through at the local grill and ordered a hamburger and fries. She knew it was not the healthiest meal for her, but she was hungry and decided she would have a light dinner. It was hard for Mary to pass up a good burger and fries.

After she arrived home, she grabbed her lunch and went inside. JJ met her at the door. He seemed relaxed, and that made Mary happy. She began thinking about her book again. She didn't know exactly how she would handle the notoriety. Mary did not like a lot of attention, and she felt a little uncomfortable. She had hoped this feeling would pass quickly.

Mary remembered she had not yet replied to David. He had not texted again, so she finally replied, "Well, isn't that unbelievable? I don't know how to handle all this, but I know God will help me however He needs to."

David comforted her by saying, "Mary, you are an amazing woman. Out of everyone I know, you can handle this. Don't be afraid."

She sent a heart emoji back and finished her lunch.

Before leaving to go back to work, she sat in her favorite chair. She stared out the window at the ocean. The weather was beautiful, and she wished she had enough time to go for a walk on the beach. What seemed like five minutes was twenty, and she was still in her chair. As she realized it was time to go back to work, she wished she could take the rest of the day off.

Mary had started her second book, and she could think of a lot of things she could write about. Instead, she drove back to work and finished her day there. She had a good day. Being busy helped her to take her mind off the uncertainty of life for a few hours.

The week went by quickly, and with Easter approaching, Mary couldn't wait to spend time with her family. Her dad and sisters were coming up for a long weekend, and she was excited. She didn't see them often, as everyone was always busy, and they lived several hours from her.

Mary had moved when she accepted her job at the inn years ago. She had to wait another couple of weeks to see them and wished she had enough room for them all to stay with her, but thankfully, she had made her dad and one of her sisters reservations at the inn. She also knew they would spend the days with her. They had not seen her new cottage or met JJ and

Sunshine. Mary was planning a lot of great meals and asked Patricia if she would make some homemade bread for her to share. Patricia was excited about doing that for Mary.

Mary had autographed copies of her new book for them, and she hoped they liked it and would be excited for her. Their time apart had been too long. She hoped they would be proud of her.

As Mary decided what she wanted for dinner, she realized she needed to eat light after the hamburger and french fries for lunch. She made a quick salad and decided she would take JJ out for a walk on the beach.

When they got to the sand, Mary had a strange thought: *Wonder if Michael will be here.* As soon as the thought came to her mind, she saw him. "I think that's him," she said out loud. "Wonder where he lives. He must be close by." He wasn't far from her and was walking in her direction. As they met, Michael looked surprised but happy. "Well, how are you, stranger?" Mary said. He had a ball cap on and looked relaxed.

Michael loved JJ and showed him a lot of attention. She loved that. "I didn't know you had a dog, Mary."

She laughed and said, "You don't know a lot about me at all, do you?"

He returned the laugh. "I guess you're right." He then asked Mary how she was doing.

She told him she'd have to go back to work on Monday, and she was tired. "The last two weeks have been eventful and almost felt like a blur."

Michael told Mary he had read her book and said how great it was. "Wow, Mary, I love your writing style. It looks like a lot of people do. I saw it made the *New York Times* best-seller list already. That is awesome!"

"Thank you so much, Michael. I am happy about what God is doing, but it's not about me at all, honestly." Mary began sharing her heart. "I don't like the attention being brought to me personally."

Michael understood what she was saying.

Mary told Michael she wished she could say she had finished his book. "But with work and everything this week, I have had limited time. I can tell you that what I have read is good, Michael. I was up late last night reading it and didn't want to put it down."

He told her he was writing his second book now.

"That's funny, Michael. I have started on my second book as well." Mary asked him how he had been enjoying his long spring and summer vacation.

He shared with her how much he loved being there and how much time he had with God. "I am usually so busy fighting the rat race of life at home, and I needed this break badly. I love the peace and quiet and the closeness I feel with Him now. It is so easy to get distracted and forget what's most important. The world kind of does that to everyone, don't you think?"

She proceeded to tell Michael how she had gotten so caught up in the world that her job had become her identity, but she had finally found a balance that gave her much peace.

Mary told Michael about her job offer two weeks ago as general manager and that Mr. Henry had offered it to her because he was sick. She then asked Michael if he would pray for Mr. Henry. "We have been claiming healing in his life."

Michael told her that he would pray for him and that he believed in healing. Michael did not even know where Mary worked or what her job consisted of, so he asked her.

"Oh, Michael, I guess you don't know, do you? I am currently the sales and marketing director at the inn. It's a gorgeous resort in town. I have been there for years and love my job so much. These last two weeks have been amazing for me, though. I took the time off to move here.

"I'm a little scared of what God is doing, though. I know I should never be afraid, but I am afraid I am being led to step out of the boat. I guess you could say I am out of my comfort zone.

"My book is selling so well, and it's all about Jesus. I don't want it to ever be about me. I don't know if I want to be a full-time author, and people are calling me to do book signings. I even had a church call me to speak. Michael, I am not a speaker. I promised Jesus I would follow Him, and this may be a huge test for me."

Michael told Mary not to be afraid. "God will give you the words to say if it comes to that, and it is His will."

Mary thanked him for being encouraging. "Michael, please pray that I walk in His ways and continue to follow Him."

Michael agreed that he would pray for her. He understood how easy it was to walk out of the will of God and live for oneself. He had spent years of his life doing that himself and knew that he could be a selfish person.

The conversation between Michael and Mary was great. He was open about his faith and transparent. He was real, and she could feel it in her heart. She sincerely hoped she was right.

JJ was obedient; he enjoyed being in Mary's arms while she petted him. However, the time had come when he was getting a little wiggly and wanted down. Mary said, "Michael, well, I guess this is our sign that it's time to get back to the cottage."

Michael giggled and said, "I guess I'd better get back too. It was so nice seeing you here today, Mary. Are we still on for tomorrow?"

"I think God had us meet today instead," said Mary. "Maybe we will continue to let Him lead our meetings. It seems our walks appear to be at the same time, as we keep running into each other."

Michael agreed. "This feels like a mystery in a way, I guess." He smiled. "Prayerfully, I will see you again if God leads it."

They said goodbye and walked away in different directions.

13

CONFIRMATIONS FROM GOD

Saturday morning came quickly, and Mary was surprised she had no plans for the day. She loved days like that. The weather was perfect, and the sky was completely blue. She thought about staying in her pajamas all day, reading Michael's book for a while, and then doing some writing of her own. She had barely started on her new book, and she knew that needed to be a priority.

Her schedule at work at the inn was getting busier; therefore, her time for writing would be limited. As she got up and did her usual daily routine, she decided to sit outside on the deck to drink her coffee and read her Bible. She was still in love with her new cottage, and it felt like the perfect home for them forever. She knew she would enjoy the day without a continuous to-do list and was happy to feel caught up a bit finally.

As she walked back inside, she thought she would check her email. As she opened her inbox, she realized she had more than one hundred messages she had not opened. As she opened each one, she became overwhelmed again. There were emails from bookstores inviting her to book signings and emails from fans asking when her new book would be out. There were many emails asking about her life and how she had gotten so close to Jesus. They wanted to know how they could accept Jesus and be saved. Mary began to cry.

Mary was overwhelmed by what God was doing, and it made her happy. "I didn't expect this," she said out loud, and she felt the Holy Spirit strongly. *This is more than I could have ever imagined*, Mary thought. *I will have to answer each one, as they are all important.*

She opened an email from a young girl named Sue. It read,

> Mary, I heard about your book and stopped on my way home to get it. I couldn't wait to read it, as everyone has been talking about it. When I got home, after dinner, I sat down and opened it. The first chapter brought tears to my eyes. I know God was speaking to me through the words on the pages. I am so sorry for the sadness you suffered as a teenager, but I want to tell you that it wasn't in vain. I faced the same situation, as my boyfriend was pushing me to have sex, and I didn't feel it was the right thing to do. Your words have saved me a lot of pain. After a lot of prayers, I broke up with him tonight because I realized he was thinking of only himself, and I wasn't going to surrender to the Enemy's will for my life. Mary, I have been set free! Thank you so much for your book. It is changing lives.
>
> Signed,
> Sue

Mary felt sad, as she knew peer pressure to have sex at a young age had become an epidemic in some way. She thought, *For the most part, this is what the world has become. Whose fault is this? Who is teaching the kids today? Why don't young boys understand the need to be gentlemen, and why don't the young girls and boys know their worth? I believe the boys are just as afraid but are trying to fit in with the others, and in some ways, they're living in the shadow, not being honest with themselves. Proverbs 3:15 says, "She is more precious than rubies; nothing you desire can compare with her."* Who teaches this to the generation of our youth?

Mary dropped to her knees and thanked God for using her pain to help others to see the truth. "Father, your Word says all things work together for our good for those who love the Lord, and I see it now, Lord. Thank you for allowing me to not live with unforgiveness in my heart but in the victory you have given me. You are my strength, Father. I don't know what will happen from here, but I know you do, as you know the number of hairs on my head. Help me with my words as I reply to these dear souls so I share only what you would have me share. Help me to continue to follow you for the rest of my days and for your glory. In Jesus's name, amen."

She got up, went back to her laptop, and continued through her emails. Each one was special and brought confirmation that she was exactly where she needed to be. As she read and answered each one, Mary wondered where God was taking her with this. *I will take this one day at a time,* she said to herself. *That's all I can handle.*

Mary spent the next few hours reading Michael's book. She enjoyed the sunshine and the breeze from the ocean as she opened the French door and went onto her deck. She was happy about the warmer weather. She loved spring, and the sound of the birds singing brought joy to her heart. *It's almost as if everything wakes up at the same time.* She had tulips coming up in a couple of places that were a surprise. Mary counted it as another gift from the Lord, as tulips were one of her favorite flowers.

She thought, *When we walk with Jesus, we begin to see everything as a gift. As our eyes are opened, we see things differently. A feeling of peace replaces fear, and we know our Savior is there with us. He comforts us in every storm of our lives, and our faith in Him begins to grow in a way that is supernatural. It is reassuring and comforting to know we have someone looking out for us. Everything may not always go the way we want it to, and it can be frustrating as we look to our flesh for the answers, but as soon as we turn back to him, we know He has great plans for us, and His plans are always the right plans.*

That thought brought one of her favorite scriptures to mind, Jeremiah 29:11: "For I know the plans I have for you, declares the Lord. Plans to prosper you and not to harm you, plans to give you hope and a future."

Mary thanked the Lord, as she had experienced that in her life for sure. She thanked the Lord that even in her weakness, He comforted her and made her strong.

As Mary looked down at her phone, she realized she had missed a call from David. She had thought about him earlier in the day and wanted to be honest with him, so she did not lead him on. She cared for him but in a friendly way and wanted to make sure he understood. She felt she was too busy now for any serious relationship, but she hoped she wouldn't lose his friendship. She hit redial and whispered a prayer: "Lord, help me say the right words to David. I don't want to hurt him in any way."

After a couple of rings, David picked up. "Hey, Mary, how are you? It's so good to hear from you."

Mary began telling him about her day and all the emails she had received. "It was so refreshing, David. People are coming to know Jesus in a personal way."

He was excited for her as he could hear her enthusiasm. David paused for a second and then asked Mary what she was doing that night.

Mary replied, "I will probably do some writing. I have had such a quiet day today, and my to-do list has finally gotten shorter, so I am taking today to do what I want to." It had been so long since she'd had a day like that.

"That's great, Mary. I was going to ask you out for dinner. I thought maybe we could go to your favorite Italian restaurant again."

Mary thanked him for the offer but said she was going to stay home that evening and enjoy JJ and Sunshine.

David sounded a little disappointed, but she felt he understood.

"Thank you for understanding, David," said Mary. She thanked him for calling, and they hung up.

After they hung up, David had a strange feeling about the call and wondered what was going on with Mary. Mary felt bad after they hung up, and she knew she needed to tell him how she felt, but she didn't want to tell him over the phone. She also didn't feel like getting dressed up to go out to dinner. She wanted to be at home for the entire day.

Mary decided to take JJ for a quick walk on the beach. He came running and somehow knew where they were going. She connected his leash, grabbed her phone and keys, and locked the door behind her. She was happy about the weather. The forecast earlier in the week had called for rain, but it had changed, and she was grateful. As they walked across the walkway to the sand, she realized she should have changed into her sandals and was still wearing her tennis shoes. "It's OK," she said. "Next time. We will have plenty of time for that, Lord willing, as the weather continues to get warmer."

Mary stopped to pick up a couple of seashells she knew were special and put them in her pockets. There was no one on the beach. Mary loved the area she was in because it was private, and she rarely saw any tourists or anyone else. They walked longer than usual, and she loved the exercise.

Mary stared out at the ocean and saw a school of dolphins swimming by. She couldn't believe it; it was the first time she had seen them. She stood at the shore and watched them jump in and out of the water. She pulled out her phone and zoomed in on the camera to try to take a picture. She got it! Three were over the water and just about to dive back in. *What a great picture*, she thought. As they swam out of sight, Mary decided it was time to start walking back to the cottage.

As she was walking back, a thought of Michael came to her mind. She wondered why she hadn't seen Michael on the beach, what he might have been doing, and if he was still enjoying his time there. She was enjoying his book and knew his heart was for Jesus. She began to pray for Michael that he would continue to find peace. She had a feeling about him that she didn't quite understand.

When they got back to the cottage, Mary thought of Patricia, so she picked up her phone and dialed her number. Patricia answered the phone but sounded tired. They talked about walking on the beach and how their days had been quiet.

"I was thinking about you. How are you? How is the baby?" Mary asked.

Patricia told Mary they were both doing well, but she had some morning sickness and was tired. "I had my checkup last Friday. Everything looks to be going well so far, thank the Lord. My first trimester will be over in a couple of weeks, so I'm hoping I feel better. I haven't been out very much and have just tried to eat healthy and get a lot of rest." Patricia asked Mary how she was.

Mary talked about her book sales and the emails she had been receiving. "I can't believe the reviews, but really, it shouldn't surprise me, as I know God gave me the words to write, but I have a feeling my life is about to change dramatically."

Patricia was happy for Mary but also felt her concern and said she would be praying for her. Mary thanked her and told her she would let her go rest. "Please call me if you need anything, Patricia."

"I will," she said, and they hung up.

Mary prayed that Patricia would feel better soon and that the Lord would protect her and the baby.

Mary began thinking about one day having children and prayed that if God wanted her to be married, He would lead her to the perfect man for her. She knew she had some time; if it were God's plan, it would happen when He wanted it to. Mary tried never to get ahead of Him, but sometimes she did and had to run back to Him quickly, or she would suffer the consequences. She continued to learn that living on her own understanding would only lead to disappointment. Repentance was a big part of her life, as patience was not her virtue.

Mary sat down in her favorite chair and picked up her laptop. She thought she would write for a while when she decided to check her email again. She was surprised when she saw that she had received more than fifty emails since she had last checked. As she began opening her emails, one really surprised her. It was from Michael. *It wasn't hard to find my email, as it was published in my book.* It read,

> Mary, I am sending you this email to let you know I am back home now. I had something come up that cut my vacation much shorter than I wanted. I was hoping to see you again by the water, but I guess it wasn't in God's plan. I wanted to send you this so you will not be worried about me or looking for me during your walks. I will continue to pray for you that you continue to be a light in this world. I pray your life stays in balance with the peace you have currently, in whatever way God leads. Meeting you was a blessing, Mary, as you inspired me in more ways than you

will ever know. In just the short time God blessed me to spend time with you, my heart turned even closer to Him. I will miss our time by the water and the conversations we had, but will keep them in my heart forever.

Your friend,
Michael

Mary was surprised when, after she read the email, a tear fell from her eye. She wondered if she had expectations about Michael she had not realized. She felt sad that she might never see Michael again and wondered why God had introduced them in the first place. He would show her.

Even when life seemed confusing, Mary had faith that the Lord was leading her. The Enemy tried to bring her fear, but He always helped her to believe, and she knew she just needed to take one step at a time. He would work it all out for His glory, and she was confident she could trust Him. She felt certain she had to follow Him, regardless of what she could see in front of her.

Mary quickly remembered Matthew 16:24: "Then Jesus said to his disciples, whoever wants to be my disciple must deny themselves and take up their cross and follow me." As she sat quietly looking out over the ocean, she wondered if she would ever see Michael again.

Her focus shifted back to the other emails, and she knew she needed to read them and send responses. As she began opening each one, she was encouraged. She read about forgiveness, lives restored, decisions of possible mistakes being redirected, love that was given when it was hard to give, fathers spending more time with their kids, and heartaches being healed.

Mary was overwhelmed by the love and grace of Jesus and knew that without Him, her book would not have been written. She thanked Him for changing hearts and lives. She began to pray. "Lord, help me to continue to be light in this dark world as I seek to follow you and to be more like you. It's only by your grace, Lord. In Jesus's name, amen."

Her phone rang, and as she looked down, she saw it was David. She picked up the call and was happy to hear from him. He began the conversation by saying, "Mary, do you have time for an early dinner?"

Mary knew she needed to talk to him. *And what better time than today?* she thought. "Of course, David. Do you want to meet somewhere?" They agreed to meet at the Italian restaurant at four.

After realizing what time it was, she decided to shower. Mary decided she would not dress up but would wear a casual pair of jeans and a cute top with sandals. She was dressed and had her makeup on when she thought about the tone in David's voice. She thought it had been a little off, but she could not decide what she was feeling. *Maybe it's nothing,* she thought. She was getting a little nervous, as she knew she had to tell him she really cared for him but wanted only to be friends.

They arrived at the restaurant at the same time, and after they got out of their cars, David came over and hugged Mary. "It's so good to see you," he said.

She agreed and prayed that God would give her the words to say.

As they sat at the table and ordered their meal, David looked at Mary and said how much he enjoyed getting to know her. What he said next caught her off guard. He told her that she had inspired him and that their time together would always be filled with great memories for him.

She gave David a confused look, as it seemed he had something else to tell her.

He said, "I am an honest person, and because we have become great friends, I want to be honest with you. I met another girl, and we have been out a few times. I told her about you and how we have become great friends. I want to focus on our time together and felt I needed to share that with you. Mary, I pray we can always be friends. You are a very special person, and I only want the best for you."

Mary was shocked but was happy she didn't have to tell him. God had it all worked out for her. *After all, He knows the plans He has for us.* She felt such relief that it was as if ten pounds had fallen from her shoulders. She cared for David but had never felt he was the one God had chosen for her long-term. She agreed they would continue to be friends and told him she was happy for him.

They talked for the next hour and laughed together. The conversations were healthy and comfortable. As they got up to leave the restaurant, their hearts were at peace.

Before going back to her cottage, she remembered she needed to shop for bedroom furniture for the guest room. She had finally unpacked all the boxes from the move, and her sister was going to stay with her when they came for a visit.

She was excited about seeing her family again and hoped they would love her cottage as much as she did. She had been looking online at local stores and found a set she loved. She set her GPS and drove to the store. As she walked in, a salesman came up to her to ask if he could help. She showed him on her phone the set she had seen, so he took her to it. It was perfect, just as she'd thought. She loved the sale price and decided that was the one. It was a distressed white antique bedroom set with a beautiful, beachy shiplap headboard. The dresser and nightstand were in the same distressed finish to match. She lay on several of the mattresses and decided on one that was medium plush. Realizing she was pleased with her choice, the salesman wrote up the ticket, and she paid for it. She was happy they could schedule the delivery for the next day.

14

FAMILY VISIT

The day arrived when Mary's sisters and dad were coming for a visit. She was excited, as it had been too long. She had already been to the grocery store to pick up all she thought she needed for her planned meals. They were going to be there for only three days, but she was grateful. They were scheduled to arrive at the cottage at about three in the afternoon, and it was close to eleven. She spent the morning cleaning and checking her email to answer any messages that had come in. She was still surprised at the responses she was getting. They encouraged her. Mary knew her time spent writing was not in vain, as God was using her book to change lives. She was comfortable in knowing that was the reason He had led her to write it and that He was in the center of it all.

Mary sat down to write for a while and decided she would write a quick poem that had come to her mind and was sketched in her heart. After she wrote and read it, she knew the words had come from Jesus. She loved how He led her writings. She had been thinking about Easter and how blessed she was to have such a personal relationship and understanding of Jesus's love for her. *So many don't have this*, she thought. It was sad for Mary to see the lostness in others, and she wondered how they ever got through life without Him.

Although she had always been taught about Jesus and had a beautiful relationship with Him, her faith had grown deeper. In the past, she had felt herself many times in complete chaos and pain while believing she was good. When she realized she wasn't good and needed a Savior, everything in her life changed. Her eyes had been opened to the truth, and He had begun setting her free from all she had been holding on to and begun healing her heart. She wrote the words the Lord gave her:

Jesus took the sin of the world.
He died for you and me.
He had to make a choice
so that we could all be free
as He spoke these words:
"Father, please take this cup from me."
He spoke again to say,
"Not my will, but your will it must be."
In His choice, He set us free—
free from fear and unforgiveness,
free from shame and guilt,
free from ourselves as we choose to repent.
His will is the only one
that brings reconciliation.
His will is the only way
that brings peace and redemption.
Today may we choose Jesus
and pray for each other
that we walk in only His light
as we walk through life together.

Before Mary knew it, it was close to two, and she was getting more and more excited about seeing her dad and sisters. They were going to come to the cottage first, and she would then take them to the inn to get checked in there. Her dad was elderly, and she was sure he would be tired from the trip.

As Mary sat thinking about their arrival, she stared out at the ocean. She began to pray. "Lord, thank you for bringing my family here for a visit.

You know my excitement, and I pray they enjoy their time here with me. It has been too long since we have been together, and I pray that our hearts are unified during this time."

The doorbell rang, and she thought they might have been early, but it was Patricia. She had been baking bread all morning. Mary said, "Patricia, it is so nice to see you. Look at you! You look great. How are you and the baby?"

Patricia responded, "I have felt great today. I am praying I'm turning a corner from morning sickness. It's been awful. I'm hoping I can start enjoying baking again, and today has encouraged me to do just that. I've missed it, so thank you. Paul has missed it, too, ha-ha. I think he's even lost a little weight, so maybe this will help me to cut back on baking as much bread in the future. Paul loves my bread, you know. Especially when it comes out of the oven and is still hot."

Mary couldn't thank Patricia enough for baking the two loaves for her and her family. "It smells amazing, Patricia. You really should open a bakery."

Patricia wanted to stay but needed to get back home. She had to clean the mess she'd left in the kitchen after time had gotten away from her; she'd wanted to get the bread over to Mary before Mary's family arrived. They hugged and said goodbye.

Mary heard a car pull into the driveway. Her dad and sisters had arrived. Her sister Beth was driving, and her dad was in the front seat. Her sister Sarah was sitting in the back seat. When they got out of the car, Mary stood with tears in her eyes. She gave her dad and her sisters big hugs. She told them she was happy to see them. The drive there had gone well, and they all were happy to be together.

JJ was excited to have company, and he couldn't stay still. He loved people, and it was obvious. They had not met JJ until that day, and it didn't take long before they loved him too. Mary invited them in. They loved the cottage and were proud of her for all she had accomplished.

Beth was the oldest and was always kind. She had a family of her own and grandchildren, so it was hard for her to get away. Sarah was always busy with her family as well and had a sassy personality. She was always the life of the party and was always fun to be around. They were both responsible and had amazing families. Mary missed seeing everyone else but was grateful to have her siblings and her dad for a few days. Her dad looked a little frailer than the last time she had seen him. She loved her dad and couldn't imagine ever losing him. She knew that day would come but prayed it would be a long time away. Mary suddenly realized how much time she had lost with them.

Mary offered her family some homemade lemonade and asked if they were hungry. They had already had lunch, so they declined food but suggested they take their lemonade onto the deck. As they walked out onto the deck, she saw her dad standing there as if he had something on his mind. Mary walked over and asked him if he was OK.

He said yes but added, "Your mama loved the ocean, Mary. When you girls were all very small, we would try to get to the beach on occasion." The ocean brought back a lot of memories to him.

Sarah talked about the time she and her mama had been riding on a raft, and a wave had come over them. She had thought they'd drown, but all had been OK.

They all began talking about memories of their mom and the vacations taken when they were young. Revisiting those memories was wonderful in many ways, but always missing their mom was still difficult.

Mary asked if they wanted to walk on the beach and if her dad felt he had the strength to walk that far. The walkway was sturdy, and it had a couple of places with benches where he could stop to rest if he needed to. They all agreed they would go. Beth and Sarah loved the beach, and both mentioned that maybe later in the summer, everyone could come together. Mary said she would love that. She also realized she needed to take the time to drive there to spend time with them more often as well.

As they walked on the beach together, Mary felt sadness. She realized time was quickly passing by and how far they had drifted apart. She knew those years could not be given back to them, and their busy lives had taken them from one another.

Her dad looked tired, and Mary realized they should head back to the cottage. She had already prepared their dinner, and it was in the oven warmer. She thought that after dinner, she would have them follow her to the inn to get her dad and Beth checked in for the night. Sarah would come back with her to sleep in the guest room. Mary knew they would have a lot to catch up on.

When they got back to the cottage, she sliced some of Patricia's bread and made garlic toast to go with her lasagna. She had already prepared a salad as well. The walk on the beach had given everyone an appetite, and it was close to dinnertime. Sarah and Beth helped set the table outside on the deck, as the evening was beautiful, and they wanted to sit outside for dinner. Mary loved that idea, as she enjoyed sitting by the water.

As everyone sat down, Mary filled four glasses with water and added slices of lemon. She made everyone a plate and took the food and drinks to them. Mary loved to show hospitality, and it filled her heart to cook for others as often as she could. This time was different. It was her family, and she couldn't have been happier. It had been years since she'd had the opportunity to serve them.

They all sat and enjoyed their dinner. The conversations were great. Mary enjoyed reflecting as discussions and reminders of their lives together were spoken. Her dad smiled a few times and laughed in a way she remembered from growing up, usually when he was doing something special for one of them. For example, he'd bought each one a car for their sixteenth birthday. The cars were not purchased new—in fact, most had been many years old—but he'd made sure they all had one, and they all loved the memories of how he brought them home to them and gave them the keys. Beth began talking about her first car and how she had wanted an orange Volkswagen Beetle. He had found her a Volkswagen, but when he bought it, it was white, so after he had gotten it home, he'd taped the glass and painted it himself with orange spray paint. Beth drove that car for a few years, and she remembered it as if it was yesterday. They all loved that story and loved their dad's heart.

The time had come to clear the dishes and get them to the inn before it was too late. Sarah unloaded her suitcase and brought it into the guest room. Sarah decided she would go with Mary. Dad and Beth followed Mary. They had never had the opportunity to see where Mary worked and were excited. As they arrived at the inn and drove down the long entranceway, they saw the beautiful flowers, Bradford pear trees, and dogwoods blooming. The drive was beautiful.

When they arrived at the entrance, an employee came out wearing a top hat, and as he tipped his hat, he welcomed them. When he saw Mary and said hello, he realized her guests must have been family and thought he needed to do an extra good job in welcoming them. Mary told him to relax and not to worry, as she was always proud of him for doing a great job. He had been an employee there for years and took a lot of pride in serving the guests. He took their luggage out of the car and gave them a valet ticket to show when they needed to pick up their car again.

Her dad didn't like a lot of fuss over him but looked at Mary and gave her a thumbs-up as if to say, "You go, girl. You have a big job." He was always proud of his girls and told them as often as he could. Beth and Sarah had great jobs, too. Beth was an executive with a large PR firm, and Sarah was a well-known Real Estate agent.

The bellman took their luggage to their rooms while Mary checked them in and got their keys. As they all got in the elevator to the third floor, where their rooms were, Mary hugged them and thanked them again for coming. They all looked happy.

The rooms at the inn were very nice, and the beds were covered with the finest linens made. She prayed that they would enjoy their time there and that the staff would take great care of them. Beth and Sarah were both happy that they also had a heated pool and hot tub. They thought they also might have a spa day together. Mary went into the spa to ask about the availability for the next day, and they had time available the next morning at nine, so she booked it. She was sure her dad had never had a massage, and she could talk him into it.

As she came out of the spa, she texted Sarah to see where she was. They were all inside the indoor pool area, checking it out, so she walked there to meet them and tell them the good news. They were excited about the massages, and her dad reluctantly agreed. Their plan was to meet back at the hotel at eight the next morning for a quick breakfast and coffee. Mary and Sarah told them they would see them in the morning and left the hotel.

As they drove back to the cottage, Sarah was quiet. Mary hoped nothing was wrong and asked if she was OK. She felt she was just tired from the trip. As they arrived back at the cottage, Mary told her to make herself at home, and she took JJ out for a quick walk.

After their walk, Mary came back inside and didn't see Sarah. She walked back to her room and realized she had put on her pajamas and was sitting on the bed.

As Mary walked into her room, she began to cry. Sarah said, "Mary! What's wrong?"

Mary told her how much she had missed her. She had not realized how much until she had arrived at the cottage.

Sarah hugged her and said, "I totally understand because I feel the same way. It's amazing how we all get so busy that we forget how important family is. We will have to change that for sure. We need to make it a point to spend more time together."

"You know you are welcome here anytime you would like to come. Now that I am not in the apartment anymore and at least have a guest room, it will be more enjoyable."

They then agreed they needed to get to bed, as they had an early morning.

Mary walked JJ for the last time of the day, slipped on her pajamas, and crawled into bed. The day had been emotional for Mary as she realized she had not taken the time she needed to be with her family. She thought again about the balance she was trying to achieve in her life and began to pray. "Father, thank you for continuing to show me where we have all failed. Thank you for bringing my family to me for the next few days. It seems everyone is so busy these days that we all forget what's important. Help us to rest well tonight in the peace that you supply us so we can enjoy the next few days together. In Jesus's name, amen."

Morning came quickly, and when Mary got up, Sarah was in the shower. "She must have been up for a while." Mary turned the coffeepot on and walked JJ outside. It was six o'clock, so they didn't feel they had to rush to the inn to meet at eight. She sat down with her Bible and started drinking her coffee when Sarah came into the living room. She looked pretty. Her blonde hair had gotten long, and she had a cute outfit on. "Hey, girl," Mary said. "Grab a cup of coffee. The cups are in the cabinet above the coffeepot."

Sarah preferred her coffee just like Mary's, with cream and their favorite, Anderson's pure maple syrup. As she walked into the living room, sipping her coffee, she said, "Yummy."

Mary remembered Sarah loved coffee, too. They sat and read together for a while and talked about how well they had slept. Mary said, "The sound of the ocean always puts me to sleep. It's peaceful, I guess."

They were both excited about their massages and wondered how their dad would like it. They both laughed, trying to figure out what his response would be after it was over. Sarah poured another cup of coffee, and they walked out onto the deck. The sound of the ocean was refreshing.

As Mary realized what time it was, she told Sarah she should shower while Sarah decided to stay on the deck to finish her coffee. Mary picked out a cute pair of capri pants, a floral top, and sandals. She quickly put on a little makeup and joined Sarah on the deck. "I think we are both excited about seeing Daddy and Beth for breakfast this morning, aren't we?"

When they arrived at the inn, Mary realized she had a text from Beth. Beth and their dad were already in the restaurant and told them they would meet them there. As Mary and Sarah walked in, the hostess knew where to seat them, knowing they were family. As they sat down, Mary could see they looked well-rested. Dad and Beth both said they had rested well and continued to talk about how nice the inn was and what great service the staff had provided. Dad told Mary, "Everyone loves you here."

She said, "I love my job and everyone here too, Dad. Thank you!" Mary had asked her dad if he was ready for his massage.

He laughed a little and said, "I guess." He had never had a massage, so they were all looking forward to hearing what his thoughts were afterward.

They ordered breakfast from the buffet, and all had a great meal. The food at the inn was prepared by some of the best-known chefs in the world. "We were very lucky to hire them—that's for sure," Mary said.

While they were eating, Mr. Henry came in. Mary introduced him to her dad and sisters. He was happy to meet them finally and was sure to tell them how many conversations they had had about them. "Mary misses you all so much. I am so happy you are here for a visit. Please know that everything you need here is on the house. The treat is mine. Make yourselves at home, and if I or my staff can get you anything, please let us know." He left them alone for breakfast and told Mary to enjoy her family.

As soon as Mr. Henry left the restaurant, her dad looked at her and said, "Mary, you are blessed. This is a wonderful place, and Mr. Henry is very nice. I am so happy we came, so I can feel some of what you share with us all the time." He looked at Mary again and said, "Dad is very proud of you, girl!"

Mary felt a tear fall from her eye onto her cheek. "Thanks, Dad!" She continued to long for her dad's approval.

They finished their breakfast, and the waiter was clearing the table when Mary said, "OK, gang, let's go pamper ourselves for a while." Mary was excited to treat her family to something special.

Four rooms were available for them to all have massages at the same time. As soon as they arrived, they were greeted by their massage therapists and were asked to come inside.

Ninety minutes felt like fifteen, and Mary fell asleep. After their massages, they met out front. Her dad looked as if he had been sleeping. Mary asked them if they'd enjoyed themselves, and they all agreed it had been wonderful. She was surprised at her dad's response when he said, "Why did I wait until I was old to do this? Oh, my goodness, I loved it!" They all laughed, and their hearts were full.

They decided to spend the rest of the day relaxing at the cottage. After lunch, her dad turned on the TV and fell asleep in the chair. Mary loved to see her dad with so much peace.

Their time together went quickly; before Mary knew it, it was time for them to leave. She was sad but grateful for their time together. It had been enjoyable. She missed her family, and they all committed to making it a priority to spend more time together.

Her dad and Beth were still at the inn, and they had agreed that Mary and Sarah would come over early as soon as they were up. Sarah's luggage was packed and loaded in the car.

Mary and Sarah had coffee together at the cottage, showered, and dressed. Mary walked JJ, and they left to meet their dad and Beth.

During their drive to the inn, Sarah told Mary how proud of her she was and that she was happy to see her faith in Jesus. "You are a beautiful light to this world, Mary," Sarah said.

Mary smiled. "Thank you for saying this, but you know how easy it is to fall, Sarah. I'm not exempt from that, either. I've realized over the years that the second I take my eyes off Jesus, I fall. Keep praying for me." They both agreed they would keep praying for each other, and they both understood how difficult life could be without Jesus. Mary knew they were blessed that the Lord had opened their eyes to the truth.

As they arrived at the inn, Beth and their dad had their luggage downstairs. They all walked into the restaurant and had breakfast together. As always, the food was delicious. Mary didn't want to say goodbye but knew she had to. As tears fell from her dad's eyes, Mary hugged him and her sisters. As they drove away, tears flowed from Mary's eyes. Her heart felt empty, as it had been too long since they had been together, but Mary was grateful for the last few days with them. She longed to be with her family. She had not made spending time with them a priority in her life because of work and everything else she had made a priority.

15

A SURPRISE FROM MICHAEL AND A BABY SHOWER

M ary arrived back at her cottage after a lovely time at breakfast with her family and decided to check her email. As she scanned through the messages to decide which one to open first, she saw one from Michael. It read,

> Mary, I have missed you. I pray you are well. It looks as if I will be coming back to the beach for a couple of months. The house I was renting is still available. I will be arriving next Friday. I hope we can get together.

Mary took a deep breath and felt a little relieved to hear from him but wondered what must have taken place for him to have to leave so quickly. She then thought, *This weekend. He's coming back.* She found herself excited, trying to wrap her mind around it. She replied to him,

Hi, Michael. It is so good to hear from you. Are you OK? You never told me why you left, and I have been concerned. However, I am looking forward to seeing you again. Call me when you get in.

She left him her number and told him to be careful traveling.

As she began reading her other messages, she was again comforted by the thought of how God was using her book and life experiences to help others. She knew her writings came from Him and was grateful He would always be there to protect her as long as she stayed close to Him. She prayed she would never forget or fall into temptation. Mary knew how quickly things could happen if she didn't keep her eyes on Jesus.

Mary spent a few hours cleaning her cottage. She hoped she could take JJ for a walk on the beach a little later.

Mary's dad called to let her know they had arrived home safely. He told her how much they'd enjoyed their trip, how much he loved her cottage, and that he already missed her. He thanked her again for the massage and said he would be coming soon for another one.

She laughed under her breath and was happy he'd enjoyed it so much. She told her dad she loved him and thanked them for coming. Before hanging up, Mary said, "I miss you already, Dad!"

She could hear sniffles over the phone when he replied, "I miss you too, Mary!"

As they hung up, she realized it was getting late, and if she and JJ were going to walk on the beach, they needed to get going. She called him over, connected his leash, and locked the door behind her. As they walked down the walkway, she started thinking about Michael. *I can't believe he will be back next Friday. I wish I knew why he left,* she thought.

She and JJ enjoyed their walk on the beach, as always. She did not find a seashell she liked this time but knew there would be many more times when she would. "The water seems a little rough today," she told JJ. "I should check the weather to see if a storm is coming in." She thought she remembered seeing rain in the forecast. The sky was a little overcast, so she decided to head back to the cottage.

As they got back to the cottage, Mary tried to decide what she wanted for dinner. She had bought a frozen pizza and thought that might be quick, so she turned her oven on and took it out of the freezer. She didn't buy frozen pizzas often, and they were not her favorite. *But tonight, it will be fine*, she thought.

Mary was happy that summer had arrived and was excited about spending her first summer in her new cottage. She already had many great memories there. She wanted to take a few days off but decided she wouldn't because she didn't want to put any pressure on Mr. Henry. He had been good to her, and she never wanted to take advantage of his kindness.

Mary had been so busy with her book and work that she had not spent a lot of time with her friends, and she was missing them. They had talked on the phone a lot, as the girls had all planned Patricia's baby shower but had not taken the time to meet in person at all.

After dinner, she decided to shower and put on her pajamas to enjoy a quiet night with JJ and Sunshine. She had the next day off and was happy about that. *I guess Michael will be here later in the week. Maybe I will invite him over and make dinner for him or something*, she thought. She was sure he would be tired from his trip. She remembered the baby shower for Patricia was the next Saturday and decided to give Patricia a call to check on her to see how she was feeling.

Her pregnancy had gone well after she got through the first trimester. She was in her eighth month, and her belly was huge. Mary thought how blessed she was and what a wonderful gift a newborn baby was. She and Paul had decided they would wait to find out the sex of the baby, but they were not sure if they could wait another month. Patricia answered the phone and sounded relaxed.

She was happy to hear from Mary and told her she had been resting since dinner and that they had the nursery almost finished. They talked about the baby shower and how excited they were about getting together for it. It was planned for next Saturday and was being held at the bakery across town in a private room they had rented. They were all excited, as they had planned a lot of fun games. They were making fun foods, and the bakery was preparing cupcakes. Twenty-five people were invited, and the RSVPs were due tomorrow. A lot of the invitees were family, and she was sure they would all be there. They talked about the baby moving so much that Patricia wasn't sleeping well. Her schedule for sleeping was during the day. She hoped that would change as soon as she was born.

Mary stopped her and said, "Patricia, did you say *she*?"

"Oh, I did," replied Patricia. "I guess we will find out soon enough, won't we?" They both giggled.

Mary then told Patricia about Michael's email and his plan to be back on Friday. Patricia asked if he was OK and if he had ever told her why he left early. Mary proceeded to tell her that he had not, but she was sure whatever it was must have been important. "Anyway," Mary said, "I think I am looking forward to seeing him."

Patricia knew Mary was beginning to care for him. She just hoped Mary would pay close attention and be careful.

Mary told Patricia she would be careful. "I'll see you on Saturday," she said. As they hung up, Mary thought about the gift she'd bought her: the softest, sweetest blanket with a plush lamb. Mary loved it, and she hoped Patricia would too. Most importantly, she prayed the new baby would love it.

The rest of the night was exactly what she wanted: a quiet night of journaling and writing. Before she knew it, it was close to nine, and she was falling asleep.

When morning came, Mary realized she hadn't slept well. She'd tossed and turned most of the night, thinking about Michael coming and Patricia's baby shower. She was excited for her but also felt a little jealous. Mary had wanted children before now. She'd thought she would be a young mom, and she didn't understand. Thoughts of Edward came back to her, and she realized that at times, she was still angry with him.

She prayed God would heal her heart continuously, as she knew her trust issues were causing her to be standoffish toward people she really cared about.

As she got out of bed, she tried to focus on her day. She needed coffee and turned it on to brew. After feeding JJ and Sunshine, she remembered the fresh eggs she had gotten a few days before and decided to scramble an egg. She had bought some fresh bread at the bakery, so she put some butter on it and put it in the toaster oven. Mary always enjoyed a great breakfast.

It was Saturday morning, and Mary sat in her favorite chair with a cup of coffee. She read her Bible for a while. While reading, she started thinking about how she had missed a few days and about what she had been doing to skip her time with the Lord. Her family had been there, and they had been busy each morning early to get to the inn for breakfast. She didn't like missing her time with the Lord and knew how important it was.

After reading, she decided she would get in the shower and then get Patricia's baby gift wrapped. She had also picked up some vegetables to make a veggie tray and a special dip to take to the shower.

Before Mary knew it, it was almost time to leave for the baby shower. She called JJ for a quick walk outside, grabbed Patricia's gift, the veggie tray, the dip, her purse, and her keys, and drove to the bakery.

When she arrived inside, Patricia was standing there admiring the cake. She looked beautiful. She had on a peach dress, and she looked like an angel. She appeared happy but a little tired. She saw Mary come in, walked over to her, and gave her a big hug. "Mary, it's so good to see you. Everyone should be here soon."

They walked over together to put Mary's tray on the table. All the food looked amazing. There was so much. The bakery had done a fabulous job on the cupcakes. They were mixed in pink- and blue-colored icing with sprinkles on top.

When the guests came in, they all swarmed around Patricia. She was loved by so many. Karen and Victoria came in together. "It is so good to have everyone together," said Mary.

Victoria had driven in from Charlotte the night before and spent the night with Karen. She and John had finally found a home there and were moved and settled in. The drive wasn't long for her, and she was happy about that. She knew she had to see her friends as often as she could. Patricia asked Karen to pray for their food, and she was happy to.

Karen prayed, "Father, we thank you for this day as we celebrate Patricia and the beautiful baby you are blessing her and Paul with. Father, as she becomes a mother, be with her and guide her and Paul as you nurture them into becoming great parents as they teach their child about you and the love you have for their family. I pray they are unified as one with you and that they continue to make you the center of their lives. May we all enjoy one another today, and may you be glorified. In Jesus's name, amen."

Mary told Patricia she would be first in line to get her food. Patricia laughed and said, "It's about time." They all laughed with her and got in line behind her. Karen had made orange sherbet punch. It was refreshing, and the food was all delicious. The cupcakes were fabulous.

After they were done eating, Mary brought out the games to play. They all had a great time. The game of wrapping toilet paper around Patricia's belly and deciding the measurement was the funniest, as no one guessed it correctly. Everyone was way off. The laughter in the room was contagious. The shower and the company were refreshing for everyone who attended.

The time came to open the gifts. Patricia sat in the center as they all sat in a circle around her. She was beautiful and full of joy. As she opened each gift one by one, Mary could see the joy and feel her gratefulness as she imagined her baby in each outfit and in the stroller, knowing each gift was going to be a huge part of her life in the days to come. Everyone was snapping pictures and enjoying the moment.

The time for the party to be over arrived, and the cleanup began. While all the guests were leaving, Mary stopped Patricia and hugged her. Mary said, "Patricia, I will always be here for you. You can count on me for conversations in the middle of the night, a shoulder to cry on, someone to laugh with, or whatever you need. You know that, right?"

Patricia said she knew, and her heart was full. She adored Mary and was grateful for her friendship.

When Mary arrived back at the cottage, she was happy to see JJ greet her at the door. She brought her things in and put them on the counter in the kitchen. Sunshine came running around the corner from the bedroom as if to say hi. Mary was tired. She sat on the couch and enjoyed the company of her fur babies. She wondered if she would ever be married and have a baby of her own.

As she thought about Patricia and all the fun they'd had that day, she also thought of the responsibilities that were changing in her life and how happy Patricia was to have Paul by her side to enjoy life with. Paul appeared to be a supportive husband, and Mary felt sure he would be a great dad as well. That made Mary happy.

Mary got up to take JJ for a walk on the beach. The weather was nice, and she wanted to take advantage of every spare second she had to enjoy the ocean. Life had become busy for her with her book and work. Little did Mary know how her life was about to change.

16

MARY'S FALL TO TEMPTATION

Morning came, and it was a new work week. Mary was up early after a wonderful night's sleep. She arrived at work a few minutes early, as she had meetings all day. She loved her job, and it helped her to keep her mind off everything else—that was until she had thoughts of Michael and the mystery of her meeting him and how he had to leave unexpectedly.

The last email she had received from Michael said he would be back on Friday. She had a few extra minutes and thought she would check her email again. She had more than two hundred new emails. She wondered how she would continue to manage them but loved reading each one. The first email was from someone sharing how Mary had encouraged her to read her Bible daily and journal her days to reflect on later.

Mary then realized she had not read her Bible that morning. She began to pray. "Father, forgive me for not taking the time out of my morning to read and journal. What is wrong with me? I have come to realize so greatly my dependence on you. Help me, Lord."

Mary thought of one of her favorite scriptures, Galatians 2:20: "I have been crucified with Christ and I no longer live, but Christ lives in me. The life I now live in the body, I live by faith in the Son of God, who loved me and gave himself up for me."

As Mary continued to read her emails, she saw another one from Michael:

Hi, Mary. It looks as if I will be arriving a little earlier than I thought, not on Friday. I will be coming in on Monday. Thanks for sending me your number. I will call you when I arrive.

She read it again and thought, *Monday? That's today. What is he up to?* She then quickly closed her email and began preparing for her meetings.

The day went quickly, and Mary scheduled two additional wedding receptions. She loved sharing with the couples her gifts of appreciation, especially the scripture that would have saved her marriage had she and Edward worked at it. She thought of Edward again and prayed he was happy and well.

After Mary arrived home, she saw she had a missed call and a voicemail from a number she didn't recognize. It was Michael: "Hey, Mary, I'm back at the beach now. It's about three o'clock. Give me a call when you get this." Mary didn't know if she should call him back right away or not, but in just a second, she hit redial. She found herself feeling anxious and wanted to know what had happened when he left so early.

Michael answered, "Hi, Mary. How are you?"

She told him she was doing well and had had a busy day at the inn. She then asked him how long he would be in town this time.

He replied, "I should be here until August. I'm so sorry I left unexpectedly before, but my mother had taken ill. She was very sick, and I lost her, Mary."

Mary's heart sank. She was sad for Michael and told him how sorry she was. He thanked her for her kindness.

Before hanging up, they agreed that with her work schedule, they would get together at Mary's cottage on Friday night for dinner. She asked if pasta sounded good.

"It's perfect, Mary. Italian food is one of my favorites."

"Sounds great," Mary said. They were both looking forward to it. She gave him her address, and they hung up.

Mary was sad for him to have lost his mom so unexpectedly and felt it must have been hard on him. She was looking forward to getting to know him better and spending the summer with him if it was the Lord's will.

The rest of the week was busy for Mary. She had appointments back-to-back. Since the COVID pandemic had gone away, finally, life was becoming more normal again, and the inn's revenue was trying to make up for the loss. Mary was reminded of what a difficult time that had been for the entire world.

Friday came quickly, and Mary took off at noon. She knew she would be rushing to try to get dinner ready for Michael, so she went by the grocery store on the way home and picked up the things she needed. She also picked up a bottle of cabernet, hoping they could enjoy a relaxing night with dinner and get to know each other better. Mary was sure he would need someone to talk to about his mom's passing. She wanted to be a friend.

After Mary returned home from the grocery store, her phone rang. It was Michael. As she answered the call, the sound of his voice warmed her heart.

"Mary, I had no idea your cottage was only three doors down from the house I am renting," he said, and she was surprised. "I think I will just walk to your place. Is six o'clock OK?"

Mary agreed that the time was great. After they hung up, she started feeling a little nervous. *Oh goodness*, she thought. *Am I really doing this?* Her thoughts quickly changed to preparing dinner.

She began making her sauce and homemade Italian meatballs. She mixed the pork and ground beef and added seasonings as well as breadcrumbs and egg. Mary always fried her meatballs before putting them in the sauce and adding the drippings to the sauce. Afterward, she started her water to boil for the pasta. She then prepared a salad and buttered bread with garlic butter to go in the oven. She was almost done with the dinner preparations.

Mary decided to change her clothes and get into something a little more comfortable but cute. She decided on a pair of simple cotton capri pants, a cotton top, and her slip-on white tennis shoes. She looked relaxed and confident.

Mary could feel butterflies in her stomach, as this was the first time, she had had a dinner date at her new cottage. She prayed that God would protect her and give her discernment with her words and choices as she enjoyed the company of a new friend.

The doorbell rang. Mary's heart felt as if it skipped a beat. It was Michael. He had walked from the beach to her cottage. He was handsome and taller than she remembered. His blond hair was perfectly combed, and he was wearing a beautiful smile. Mary felt something in her heart for him, but she wasn't sure what it was. Mary smiled and welcomed him into her cottage. JJ ran to greet him as well. He said, "Hi, Mary and JJ. It's so good to see you both again." He handed her a single red rose and a bottle of cabernet.

Mary loved the rose and wondered what the significance of it was. She had already opened the bottle of wine she had bought and had two crystal glasses out on the counter. Michael hugged her and thanked her for inviting him over. He then giggled, saying, "That was a short walk to get to you."

Mary smiled and asked him which house he was in. When he told her, she quickly said, "You are close. I know that one well. I love that house and always admire it when we are walking."

Mary told Michael she had everything prepared and had to put the bread in the oven. She asked if he was hungry now or if he wanted to have a small glass of wine before dinner. He agreed that a glass of wine first would be great, so she said, "We can sit and catch up a bit."

Mary poured two glasses of wine, and they sat down in the living room. Michael said, "Cheers, Mary. I am happy we are together again."

Mary surprised herself when she said, "Cheers, Michael. Ditto to that."

Mary had grown up believing wine was not acceptable for Christians, and she wondered where that idea came from, as Jesus's first miracle had been changing water into wine at a wedding celebration. John 2:10 says, "Everyone brings out the choice wine first and then the cheaper wine after the guests have had too much to drink; but you have saved the best till now." She also remembered Ephesians 5:18: "Do not get drunk on wine, which leads to debauchery. Instead, be filled with the spirit."

It had taken Mary until her adult life to discern the difference, and she had come to the realization that a glass or two of wine over hours was not a sin. She was always comfortable with that in her spirit. She never had a good feeling about having more than that. That was where she drew the line. Discipline and personal choice were key, she thought. She prayed she would always honor her choice to be disciplined.

The conversation between Michael and Mary felt healthy and responsible. Michael shared with her how his book was selling. The interest in his book had not been what he'd hoped it would be, but he was satisfied with the revenue so far. "People are talking about it. That makes me happy." He asked Mary how she was handling all the publicity for her book and how the book signings were going.

Mary said, "It is exciting! It almost feels like a full-time job at this point. With my position at the inn and starting on my second book, I do not have a lot of extra time, but the encouraging words from everyone have been so rewarding. I could never hire anyone to handle my emails because I feel they are written for me, and I do not ever want to ignore the time people spend encouraging me. I see it as a gift for sure. Everyone is now asking about my second book. They want to know the rest of the story. It is very exciting! I am adjusting for sure. I love how this turned out, as I am pleased God is using my book to change lives. Sometimes it's exhausting, though."

Michael told Mary how proud of her he was and said he felt she would be a full-time author in God's time.

Before they even realized it, their wine glasses were empty. Mary got up to put the bread in the oven. She placed the salad and pasta on the table. Michael grinned and said how wonderful everything looked. She had thought about lighting a candle but didn't want to send the wrong message.

The conversation at dinner was nice. They talked about his mom's passing, Mary's family's visit, Mr. Henry's health, and the inn, and they talked about each other and how happy they were to have met, as well as how strange it was how they'd met—an innocent walk on the beach.

Dinner was delicious. Mary was a great cook. She loved cooking and serving others. It was a gift God had given her.

After dinner, they went back to the living room, and Michael sat by her. After he was seated, he reached for her hand, asking for permission to hold it. Mary felt a tug in her heart, as this was all new to her.

Mary longed for someone to love her, and she loved the way she felt around Michael. She was comfortable and felt like herself. She felt he cared for her exactly as she was. Michael was kind, and he seemed to show gratefulness through his actions in a real way. She loved the respect he always seemed to give her, or that was how it appeared anyway.

As they sat and talked about their lives, she could feel an emotional bond developing. They seemed to have a lot in common, and they laughed together a lot. There was also occasional sadness in their hearts from conversations that took them both to memories that were not as pleasant in their lives. Mary also knew communication was important. She liked the fact that they seemed to be able to talk about everything.

It was getting late, and Mary was tired from working all day. She decided it was time to end the night and politely told Michael. She asked him if he wanted to walk with her to take JJ out for the last time that night, and he agreed. JJ was sleeping on the floor next to her feet, so she woke him gently and told him they were going outside. Michael gently reached for her hand, and they walked outside. The night was beautiful, and the stars were shining brightly. They both stopped and looked up at the stars and thanked the Lord for such a beautiful night.

Michael began walking out toward the beach to go back home, and Mary surprised herself by asking if he wanted to come over tomorrow night for dinner as well. He agreed and asked if he could bring two steaks; he would grill for them. She loved the idea of someone grilling for her and agreed that would be perfect. She said she would make baked potatoes, a small salad, and her favorite dessert. It would be a surprise. Michael kissed her on the cheek and thanked her again for a special night. He said, "Good night, Mary," and he began walking away from her.

Mary walked back in with JJ and began putting the dishes away.

Morning came quickly. She was happy it was Saturday. She didn't want to be in any rush at all that morning and hoped she could write a little. She got up, took JJ out for a quick walk, and grabbed a cup of coffee. She then sat down in her favorite chair and read her Bible. She thanked Jesus for always being with her and for her life. She felt blessed. She then journaled for a while and wrote about Michael and their time together. How special she thought he was, and she felt their friendship was growing into something a lot deeper. She wondered what would happen when the summer ended, and he had to leave. "What will happen then?" She knew she'd better take everything slowly.

The afternoon came quickly, and she was still in her pajamas. She loved days like this when she could enjoy her day exactly as she wanted to, relaxing and writing. She walked into her bedroom and pulled out clothes to wear. She decided on a cute light blue cotton dress and sandals.

After she dressed and put on her makeup, she decided to take JJ for a quick walk on the beach. While walking, Mary looked down and saw the most beautiful seashell she had ever seen. It was as if the Lord had placed it there for her. It was shaped like a heart and had worn edges where it had been tossed over and over in the ocean. She picked it up with a beautiful smile on her face, thanking Jesus for always reminding her He was with her.

After they got back inside from their walk, she decided to get the baked potatoes in the oven, make her favorite dessert, and prepare the salad. She was excited about seeing Michael again, and he would be there within a couple of hours.

Time went by quickly, and she heard the doorbell ring. Michael had on a pair of shorts, a knit dress shirt, and sandals. He looked handsome, as usual. He reached out to her, put his arms around her, and kissed her on the cheek. He handed her another single rose and said, "It's so good to see you, Mary!"

Michael made himself at home, and she loved that. She set the table for dinner. He had already marinated the steaks for the grill. They poured themselves glasses of wine and sat out on the deck. JJ lay by her feet. They laughed a lot together, telling stories from their lives, and she believed they purposely avoided any conversation about his leaving after the summer.

Michael grilled perfect steaks and made a lemon garlic butter sauce to pour over them. Mary brought over the baked potatoes and butter and the salad. He then asked Mary what the surprise dessert was, because he was not going to finish his potato if it was something he was sure to love. She laughed and said, "I'll show you."

She got up from the table, went to the refrigerator, put her hands behind her back with the dessert, and said, "Close your eyes." He laughed and closed his eyes, and she placed a perfect cheesecake with fresh strawberries on the table. She then said, "You can open your eyes now."

He looked at the cheesecake and said, "I think I will save a lot of room for that, Mary. You went way out of your way. That looks delicious!"

She told him the story of Mr. Henry bringing her a cupcake for breakfast with a sparkler on top and saying she deserved chocolate for breakfast. "Maybe we deserve cheesecake before dinner."

They both laughed, and he said, "Let's do it." It was a special time. Cheesecake before a steak sounded like a perfect night.

After dinner, they decided they would take a walk on the beach. JJ wouldn't go this time. It was getting dark, so they grabbed a flashlight on the way out. As they began walking, Michael gently reached for her hand. They walked toward the ocean together.

The sky quickly turned into night, and the stars were shining brightly. There was a full moon, and it gave them some light. The reflection on the water from the moonlight was pretty. Michael stopped Mary, looked into her eyes, and leaned in to kiss her.

Mary pulled away. "Well, it's gotten very dark; we'd better head back now."

The mood changed quickly, and Michael obviously felt resistance. He pulled her back to him and said, "You can trust me, Mary."

She hugged him and said, "Thank you, Michael." They began walking back to the cottage and said goodbye.

Neither made plans to see each other again, and it was OK with Mary. She needed some time to adjust to the new changes she was facing. After she got back inside, she finished cleaning the kitchen and then crawled into bed.

Sunday morning arrived, and the sound of thunder roared as she woke up. The forecast was calling for a 90 percent chance of rain and possible thunderstorms throughout the day. She was happy about a rainy day, as she knew that would give her a day of rest, and she could write most of the day.

As Mary sat up in bed, she stretched. She knew she would have a busy week at work starting Monday, and she had a book signing on

Saturday. Thankfully, it was close by, and she didn't have to travel. Her book signings were great; the lines started before she arrived. She never liked turning anyone away, so she was always late in leaving. She was still overwhelmed by the attention her book was getting, but she was happy about it. Most importantly, lives were being changed as Jesus tugged on readers' hearts.

She had not had a call from Michael, and she was OK with that. She did sometimes think about their time together and how much she enjoyed it.

Monday arrived, and she was sitting at her desk when someone walked in with a beautiful bouquet of fresh flowers. The delivery person asked if she was Mary and set them on her desk. Mary was surprised. She felt sure they were from Michael.

She opened the envelope. The card read,

> Mary, I am sending you these beautiful flowers because they remind me of you. You are so beautiful. Thank you for such a great weekend. I loved every second I had with you. I felt resistance when I tried to kiss you, so I am going to let you make the next move. If you would like to see me again, call me. I will be praying for that phone call. Have a beautiful week, and know that I am thinking about you.
>
> Love,
> Michael

Mary had never wanted him to feel pushed away, but she also knew she needed to protect her heart above all else. She had not done a good job of that in the past. After all, she knew who loved her unconditionally and was truly happy with that. The Lord would help her get more comfortable in His time if it was His will.

Mary had a busy week at work, and she was happy she was able to spend some time with Mr. Henry. He had had a setback but is much better now. The doctors felt the treatment was working and hoped he would have a full recovery. Mary was still praying for healing for Mr. Henry.

Thursday came, and she had not called Michael. She sat at her desk and realized she had not thanked him for the flowers, so she picked up her phone and called.

Michael answered. "Hi, Mary."

"Hi, Michael. Thank you so much for the flowers; they are so beautiful. I have had a busy week and wanted to call to thank you before now. I also wanted to ask if you wanted to come for dinner on Friday."

He was happy she had called and said, "Mary, I would love to. What would you like to eat? I know you will be working, and I will be happy to make dinner for you this time." He asked if she liked chicken marsala and said he had a great recipe.

Mary agreed that sounded great. He asked if it would be OK if he just brought everything over and made it there. He thought it would be nice if they hung out together while he cooked, but she had to promise she wouldn't do anything. He wanted to make dinner for her and keep it simple.

Mary loved the idea of someone cooking for her and agreed it would be perfect.

"Is six o'clock OK with you, Mary?"

She agreed the time would be great.

Michael spent the next morning with his normal routine of walking on the beach and writing. He knew he would have the afternoon to pick up everything he needed to prepare their dinner, and he wanted Mary to be happy with it. He almost felt a little nervous, as Mary had captured his heart, and he didn't want to lose her.

Mary wondered if Michael knew what he wanted out of life, as he seemed to travel more than most. He never stayed in the same place for long. She wondered what he might have been running from.

Mary had a busy afternoon at the inn with new clients and was pleased with her week. The inn seemed to be back to normal, and Mary loved it. Her schedule was open after four, so she decided to leave an hour early. She wanted to freshen up and take care of JJ and Sunshine before Michael arrived at six.

When she got home, JJ looked as if he didn't feel well. He seemed to be moving slowly. She called him to her, and he didn't come. She was upset, as she had never seen JJ like that. She picked up her phone to call the vet to see if she could bring him in. The office told her to come in. She quickly picked up the phone to call Michael. When he answered, Mary told him she might have to cancel their dinner, as JJ was sick and she was on her way to the vet.

He responded, "Mary, I'm so sorry. Can I meet you there?"

She said, "If you would like to, you can."

When she arrived at the vet with JJ, the staff were waiting for him. Michael had arrived as well. The vet took him back and took his temperature; he had a low-grade fever. After doing a thorough check, the vet figured out he had a kidney infection and put him on an antibiotic.

"He will be OK," the vet said. "Be sure he is drinking, and let me know if he doesn't get better in a couple of days."

Michael followed Mary home, and they went inside. He asked Mary if she still felt up for dinner, and she agreed that if he was cooking, she could sit with JJ and watch him make a mess in the kitchen. He laughed.

"That will be nice, Michael," Mary said.

Mary walked JJ for a minute and gave JJ his medicine. She tried to feed him, but he didn't eat as usual, so she laid him on his bed. He was comfortable, so Mary got up to show Michael where everything was in the kitchen. He made her promise not to get up to help at all. She giggled and said, "OK, I promise."

Mary went back into the living room and picked JJ up to lie with her on the couch. She felt a little awkward about letting Michael do all the cooking, but he wanted to, and she liked that. She enjoyed watching him from the living room as he fumbled, trying to find things.

The house smelled good, and Michael looked like he was enjoying himself. As she looked toward the kitchen, it appeared that everything was almost ready. He brought her over a glass of wine and toasted to JJ getting well and to a new beginning for Michael and Mary. Mary liked that!

Mary was beginning to really like the idea but continued to think about what would happen after he left for the summer. Michael found a couple of candles on the counter and moved them to the table. As he lit them, he called Mary over to the table.

As she sat down, he placed chicken marsala and pasta on her plate.

He'd baked frozen garlic bread, and he made a funny comment: "Sorry, I can't make bread as you do."

She laughed and said, "It's OK, and I would be concerned if you came over with freshly baked bread that you made."

He laughed and said, "No worries. That will never happen."

He poured her another glass of wine, and they enjoyed their dinner. Michael was a great cook. That made Mary happy, too. The conversation was always pleasant with Michael.

Michael shared about his first marriage and how it had failed. His wife's family had moved across the country, and she had not wanted to be away from them. Michael had not wanted to be so far away from his mom, and they had been unable to make it work. Mary thought of Matthew 19:5: "For this reason, a man will leave his father and mother and be united to his wife, and the two will become one flesh." Mary resisted asking him why he hadn't gone to be with his wife.

Michael's life was confusing to Mary, and she decided that instead of guessing, she would ask him. His response startled her: "Mary, I didn't want to get into too many details or defile her with my words, but she also had an affair. She broke my heart, and I couldn't trust her any longer. We were very young."

Mary understood completely and told him about her story with Edward. He felt sad for Mary, as he understood what she felt. He was glad he had told her the complete truth.

They got up from the table and hugged each other. Mary kissed Michael, and before she could even think about what was going on, the moment got away from them, and it happened. She loved the feeling of being close to him, and it was a feeling she had not had since she was married to Edward.

Mary immediately realized what she had done. She said to herself, *I thought I had learned my lesson, and I have shared this very subject with other young girls! What have I done?*

Mary began to cry, and her heart was broken. *How did I let this happen?* she thought. She looked at Michael and said, "This can't happen again. Michael, I have broken God's heart. I know the truth; how did I allow this to happen?" She was kind to Michael but asked him to leave.

He understood and said, "I'm sorry, Mary," and he left.

She began to pray. "Father, please forgive me, as I have failed you. Lord, I love you, and I think of Peter in John 21:17: 'The third time he said to him, Simon son of John, do you love me? Peter was hurt because Jesus asked him the third time, do you love me? He said, "Lord, you know all things; You know that I love you."' Please forgive me, Lord."

Mary didn't take any calls from Michael for a couple of weeks. She was angry with him, and she was angry with herself. She was heartbroken that she had failed God. She knew the truth. She knew the Enemy came to kill, steal, and destroy. *How did I give in to this temptation?* she thought. Then she remembered she had not been reading her Bible every day. She wasn't praying as she had been. Mary had gotten comfortable with her life and had begun drifting away from God.

She remembered John 15:5: "I am the vine; you are the branches. If you remain in me and I in you, you will bear much fruit; apart from me, you can do nothing."

Mary began to pray. "Lord, I have failed you. How is it that I believe I am strong without you? How is it that I have failed you after all my time with you? Please forgive me, Lord. Please!"

Mary repented of her sins and was forgiven. After all, the Lord knew the beginning of one's life to the end. This was not a surprise to Him. She remembered a beautiful scripture in God's Word that comforted her and brought her much peace, 1 John 1:9: "If we confess our sins, he is faithful and just and will forgive us our sins and purify us from all unrighteousness."

Comforting Mary, Jesus also said, "Mary, in my Word, Romans 8:28 says, 'And we know that in all things God works for the good of those who love him, who have been called according to his purpose.' Mary, do you think this surprises me? I know the beginning of your life to the end. I know your heart, and you have genuine remorse. I forgive you, Mary. Follow me."

Mary loved the compassion of the Lord, and He knew her heart. She prayed again. "Father, help me daily to be more like you. Please continue to carry me through the rest of my days. In Jesus's name, amen."

Mary was scared. Her cycle was a few days late. She called her friend Karen and asked if she could come over. Karen said, "Mary, are you OK?"

"No, I'm not. I need to talk to you."

"Yes, I will be there in just a few minutes. I haven't talked to you in a couple of weeks. What's going on, Mary?"

"Please let me tell you when you get here."

In only a few minutes, the doorbell rang, and it was Karen. Mary was sobbing when she got there. "Karen, I have sinned against God. What am I going to do? I have asked Him to forgive me, but how could I let this happen?"

"Oh, Mary, come here." Karen hugged her friend and reminded her that nothing could separate her from the love of God. "He loves you, Mary. Tell me what's going on. I haven't talked to you in a couple of weeks, and I have been wondering what was going on. I'm sorry I haven't called you. We all get caught up in our own lives and forget others. I am so sorry, Mary."

Mary told her what had happened with Michael. "I know better, Karen. Why did I do that? Michael's been calling every day for two weeks, and I haven't answered his call. I can't. My life seemed to be going so well, and now look what's happened."

Karen reminded Mary that she was forgiven and that the Lord had great plans for her. Karen was a great friend, and Mary had been a great friend to Karen as well. Karen said, "Mary, I can never repay you for being there for me when God asked me to trust Him to leave my career and for the comfort you gave me. I will never forget your prayer for me. Remember when you said you trusted God until Wednesday, and He showed up on Thursday, Mary? He answered that prayer for me too. It was on a Wednesday. I will never forget that conversation. Second Peter 3:8 says, 'But do not forget this one thing, dear friends: With the Lord, a day is like a thousand years, and a thousand years are like a day. His timing isn't our timing, is it?' You can trust God, Mary. He will never leave you or forsake you."

Mary knew that she didn't feel worthy of His love for her.

Mary knew with all her heart that Jesus loved her and that He made all things beautiful. Ecclesiastes 3:11 says, "He has made everything beautiful in its time: He has also set eternity in the human heart, yet no one can fathom what God has done from beginning to end."

Mary felt peace and knew that God would use her life to bring a great testimony for His glory. Somehow, He always seemed to make everything beautiful. She knew that regardless of the outcome, He was with her and loved her.

Mary had not talked to Michael and felt terrible about ignoring his calls.

As she sat at her desk, she got a text from Patricia. Paul was taking her to the hospital. She was in labor. Mary sent a group text to the girls to be sure they were all aware of the news. Everyone was excited. It was only a day away from her due date. Patricia was ready. She had the nursery completely done and was impatient to find out the sex. She and Paul would be happy with either a boy or a girl. They were grateful and prayed for a healthy baby.

The girls agreed to stay in touch and give any updates. Paul would text to let them all know the details of the progress.

17

A BEAUTIFUL BLESSING

Mary was happy but needed a day of rest. She had not felt well all week, and she attributed it to the stress she had put on herself. Mary decided to text Victoria and Karen to ask if they wanted to get together on Saturday. They could hang out and be together—maybe grill hamburgers or something and keep it simple. They all agreed that one o'clock on Saturday would be a great time.

Friday night came, and Mary sat quietly with JJ and occasionally Sunshine, who played with her ball, chasing it across the floor, and then came up purring as if to bring comfort and much-needed love. Mary loved her life. She thought about Michael and how rude she had been to him. She was running from him, and she knew it, so she picked up the phone to call.

Michael picked up the phone on the second ring. "Mary, are you OK? I have been so worried about you." He apologized and told her he had not meant for any of that to happen.

Mary just sat quietly and listened for a few minutes. She began to cry as she felt bad about the way she had treated him. She told Michael how sorry she was, too. She hadn't stopped him and could not blame him completely.

She began comforting Michael with the words the Lord had comforted her with. "Michael, it's all going to be OK. God makes everything beautiful in His time." Mary wondered then if she had known what she was doing and if somewhere in her heart, she wanted a family, a baby, so badly that she'd allowed it.

He wanted to see her again and asked if it was possible for them to see each other over the weekend. She told him Patricia was in labor, and the girls were coming over on Saturday. "Maybe Sunday we can get together in the afternoon. Is that OK?" she said.

Michael agreed and said he would call her. When Mary hung up, she felt better. She felt at peace and was happy she had finally talked to Michael.

The girls got a group text from Paul that they'd had a baby girl. Patricia was doing well, and the baby was perfect. She weighed eight pounds, two ounces, and was twenty-two inches long. They had named her Faith. Patricia loved the name, Faith, as she had prayed that God would give her and Paul a healthy baby, and He had answered their prayers. Paul was a great husband; she felt he would be an amazing dad. Their lives had changed, and having baby Faith in their lives was a beautiful blessing. They would learn to navigate their days in the future as they leaned on Jesus for His strength and peace.

Everyone was excited. The girls agreed they would give Patricia, Paul, and the baby a few days at home together before visiting but asked Paul to please let them know if there was something they could do to help. He agreed he would and promised to send pictures.

It was close to one o'clock, and the girls were on their way. Mary needed them, and they knew it. She was blessed to have them. After they arrived, they talked about baby Faith and how happy they were for Patricia and Paul. Their lives were changing, and they knew their would-be trials, but they would work through them together.

Karen then told Mary she had brought something over for her. She said, "You know I love you, which is why I'm doing this, and no matter the outcome, we will always love you and be there for you." She handed Mary a pregnancy test.

Mary began to cry. "Seriously, Karen, what do you think? What in the world would I do?" Mary took a deep breath and was comforted by Psalm

139:13–14: "For you created my inmost being; you knit me together in my mother's womb. I praise you because I am fearfully and wonderfully made; your works are wonderful; I know that full well."

Mary took the test and went into the bathroom. She waited a few minutes, and before she read the test, she asked Karen and Victoria to come in there with her. As soon as they got in, she looked down: the test was positive. Mary was pregnant.

Mary surprised herself when she found a smile on her face, and the girls held her. Emotions changed quickly as Mary thought about how this would change her life.

She felt a surge of fear. She asked her friends, "What if I'm not a good mom? What if Michael isn't who I thought he was, and I'm a single mom?"

Karen hugged her friend and said, "Mary, in Isaiah 41:10, Jesus says, 'So do not fear, for I am with you: do not be dismayed, for I am your God. I will strengthen you and help you; I will uphold you with my righteous right hand.'"

Mary cried, realizing how much Jesus loved her, no matter what, and He promised He would never leave her or forsake her. She found comfort in the truth and knew that no matter what, He would help her.

Mary told the girls she had finally talked to Michael, and he was planning to come over tomorrow. "I guess I will tell him then." She had no idea how he would handle the news, but she had to tell him; she knew that.

The girls spent the afternoon together and, as always, had a great time. This time was a little different, though. The uncertainty in Mary's heart was real, and she felt it. They grilled hamburgers and talked about how life was changing for all of them. They talked about Mary's book and how God was using it to change lives. She wondered how this part of her story would be. She prayed that she and Michael would be husband and wife and that she would have the marriage she always had dreamed of. *Regardless*, she thought, *I know my Father will be with me.* She was beginning to realize her strength again, and that made her happy. She would lean on many scriptures to help her, and Philippians 4:13 would be one of them: "I can do all this through Christ who strengthens me."

Mary thought, *No matter how you plan your entire life out in your mind, it never seems to work out the way you had it planned. I never would have dreamed I would be in this situation. God knows all things.* She was blessed regardless. *Life can be difficult to navigate.*

"Praise God, we all know Jesus. He never promised our lives would be easy. He just promised He will never leave us or forsake us, and if we have a personal relationship with Him and ask Him to come live in our hearts, we will be saved, and we will live for eternity with Him," Mary said. "Our testimony should never be about us but about Christ. I've come to the conclusion that it's not about what we do right but how much love and compassion He has for us anyway. All have fallen short, and none are like Jesus."

They all agreed they would keep the news of Mary's pregnancy to themselves for a while and not tell Patricia either. They wanted to give Patricia and Paul some time to enjoy their new life together and have a bonding time with baby Faith.

The afternoon passed, and it was time for them to leave. Mary didn't want to be alone but knew she was never alone; Jesus was always with her.

After the girls left, Mary found herself dreaming of a new baby in her life and how much she would love being a mom. She wanted to be a great mom but didn't have any idea what that would entail. She thought of everything from the first year and prayed that God would help her. Most importantly, she hoped the baby would be healthy and happy.

Sunday came quickly, and Michael would be arriving in the next hour. She couldn't imagine how she would tell him, but she wouldn't be shy about it. She didn't have a choice and knew she would find out what kind of person he really was with this news.

The doorbell rang, and it was Michael. When he walked in, he could see that Mary was troubled. As she closed the door behind him, Mary asked if she could get him something to drink. He asked for a glass of homemade lemonade if she had any made. She always kept it in the refrigerator, so she went to the kitchen and poured him a glass. She sat beside him and said, "We need to talk."

He looked a little concerned, as he thought she was going to tell him she didn't want to see him again. But what Mary had to say was a little more intense than that, and she was sure he wasn't ready for what she had to share with him.

Mary decided just to say it, so she did. "Michael, I'm pregnant."

He took a deep breath and said, "You're what?"

"I'm pregnant," Mary said again.

He didn't speak for a few minutes. He got up from the couch and walked to the window, looking at the ocean. He had not expected that from Mary. He came back, sat by her again, and saw that she had tears falling down her cheeks. "Mary, you are so busy now, and we aren't married. Your new book, your second book, and your job at the inn. How will you manage all of this?" he said, seeming to put all the responsibility on her, as if he would not be there to help.

She became scared and didn't like where the conversation was going.

He said, "This is not good timing, Mary." He asked her what she thought of abortion.

She looked at him and said, "You don't know me at all, do you? No! I would never do that! Are you serious? Obviously, I didn't know you at all. You're so charming, aren't you? Until something comes your way that you can't deal with. This is your responsibility too, Michael. I didn't get this way by myself, you know!"

He then mentioned adoption.

Mary began to cry. "This is not going at all the way I hoped it would. I can't believe you! I can't believe you would suggest either of the options you have given me. I am surprised at you, Michael. Nothing like taking responsibility for your actions, is there? You want to sweep them under the rug and pretend this didn't happen. Well, guess what? It did!

"No worries, though. I have an amazing God who loves me, and I know He has great plans for me. If it's His will that I have a baby and become a single mom, I pray that my testimony be used for His glory and help someone else. You are not the person I thought you were, and I am happy God has shown me that. I will not get another divorce, and if it's His will that I will be a single mom, then so be it." She walked to the door, opened it, and said, "You can leave now."

Weeks went by, and Mary balanced her life as best as she could. She was busy with work and the popularity of her book, as well as doing as much writing as she could to finish her second book. She was now going into her second trimester. She had become comfortable with the idea of being pregnant and was even excited about it. She had shared the news with Mr. Henry, her friends, and her family. They all were supportive of her, as they knew Mary's heart.

Mary had become consumed with eating healthily and exercising. Everything she did was with the thought of her new baby growing inside her. The girls were always encouraging, and it helped that she had baby Faith to spend time with. Patricia and Paul were still adjusting to their new life as parents and other than Jesus, Faith had become the center of their lives. Mary was learning a lot from Patricia, as she was a great mom. Mary found herself spending as much time as she could with them.

Mary had not heard another word from Michael. She had come to the realization that, sadly, he would not be in her life. She hated that for the baby, but she would share that their Father was in heaven, and she would do the best she could to make up for both. She knew it would never be the same, but that was her life now, and what else was she going to do? Mary continued to strive to do the best she could, and she knew the Lord was her strength.

Mary had always had a heart for single moms and had had no idea she would ever be one. Although her heart was broken about her baby's lack of a father figure in life, she was more than happy that, prayerfully, she would have a baby she could love unconditionally. She knew she would do everything she could to give her baby the best life she possibly could. She began to see her new life as a gift. After all, God's Word was clear: a baby was fearfully and wonderfully made, a gift from heaven! Was the situation what she preferred for her and the baby? No. Would she receive the situation she was in as a positive and do the best she could? Yes! Her baby was a gift from God, and she would be the best mom she could be. She would only be judged for her actions. God would judge Michael.

Mary's doctor's appointments all went well. The baby was growing perfectly, and the heartbeat was strong. Mary felt the baby move, and it preferred to move a lot at night, keeping her awake. She was getting tired from not resting enough, but she was happy. She had to be.

She wanted to know the sex of the baby, and finally, she had an appointment where, if all went well, she would find out. Victoria and Karen wanted to go with her for support, so they met there. During the ultrasound, the nurse wanted to know if she was ready to know the sex of her baby. "Yes," she replied. Her heart almost skipped a beat in anticipation of knowing.

"It's a girl, Mary. She looks like a perfectly healthy little girl."

Mary cried, and her friends came over to her and held her hand as if to say they loved her. She knew they were the greatest friends a girl could ever have had, and she was grateful.

Work was going great, and Mary was going into her third trimester. She was getting tired during the day now. She rested more in the evenings after work and before bed.

Mr. Henry had finally beaten his cancer, and she could not thank God enough for healing him. She needed him and his friendship. He was supportive of Mary, and she knew she could count on him.

Her family was also supportive of her, and they were all excited about the baby coming soon. They were all waiting for the call and promised that as soon as they knew, they would get in the car to be there with her. Karen had agreed to take JJ home with her for a few days so Mary could focus on the baby.

Mary had been busy getting the baby's nursery set up. She tried hard not to see the negatives of her doing it by herself. As she sat on the floor with the instructions and what seemed like a million parts, including bolts, screws, springs, and rails, she began putting the crib together. She had bought one that could be changed into a toddler bed when the baby outgrew the crib. Before she could catch herself, she was sobbing. She was sad—not for herself but for the baby. This was not at all what she had expected her life would be like as she had envisioned a perfect Christian family building a life together.

Her guest room had become the nursery in her little cottage. She painted the room a pale yellow. It reminded her of a happy, peaceful place. *Like sunshine*, she thought. The baby would bring much joy into her life. She wanted her daughter to grow up with so much joy and peace that her life felt perfect. She knew that thought was unrealistic, but she prayed her daughter would never have pain and would always feel secure. Regardless, she knew she would do her best.

She finally got the crib together. It was beautiful. She hung a mobile above the bed. These were precious moments. The mobile played sweet lullaby music. Mary tried to think of everything her daughter would love and felt so much love for her. Although she had not met her yet, she had bonded with her and knew her every kick and movement.

The girls planned a baby shower for Mary. The shower was on Saturday at two in the afternoon. They chose the same private room at the bakery where they'd had Patricia's shower, as everything had worked out so well for her. Reflecting on Patricia's shower, Mary realized a significant difference: Patricia was married, and Mary was becoming a single mom. She knew life would be a little more difficult for her, but God would give her the strength she needed. She was confident of that.

Saturday came, and it was time for Mary to be at the baby shower. As she drove over, she felt a little lonely and began to pray. "Father, I know you are my strength. You are my security. You promise you will never leave me or forsake me. Please be with me and the baby today and help us to enjoy what my dear friends have planned for me. Thank you, Father, for giving me such great friends. In Jesus's name, amen."

As she walked in, Victoria, Karen, and Patricia were already there. They had the room decorated nicely. This time, all the cupcakes were pink, with glitter on top. The guests began coming in; however, she missed her sisters. They would come as soon as she went into labor, but they hadn't been able to get away for the shower. Her sister Beth had crocheted a beautiful, large baby blanket with the softest thread she had ever felt. She knew it would be a forever blanket the baby could always cherish. Beth had mailed her a beautiful bassinet in white lace that she could keep by her bed for a few weeks until Mary was comfortable putting the baby in her crib.

Before the food was served, Patricia asked if she could pray. "Father, thank you for our dear friend Mary. Thank you for bringing her into our lives. She has been an amazing friend to all of us, and our lives would not be the same without her. Lord, we ask that you be with Mary and the baby, and may their lives be filled with peace and joy that we know only you can provide. In Jesus's name, amen."

As always, the food prepared was wonderful. Mary loved the buttercream icing on the cupcakes and made sure she had at least two. She had managed to keep her weight where she should have, and the doctors were all pleased.

The shower was a lot of fun, and Mary got everything she needed for the baby and more. She was excited for the baby to come. Their rented time allotted for the room was up, and they knew they needed to begin cleanup. Everyone hugged Mary, and they all said they would be praying for her.

"Time goes so fast," said Mary. She was due within the week and planned to take six weeks off for maternity leave.

Her last day of work had come, and Mr. Henry was happy to give her the time off and more if she felt she needed it. He'd hired an intern to help her through the time when she would be off. It was noon, and Mary planned to leave early on her last day. Mr. Henry helped Mary get everything to the car, hugged her, and told her he would be praying for her. He made her promise she would let him know when she went into labor. She promised, giggled, and said, "See you later, Mr. Henry. Don't be a stranger." He assured her he would not be.

Victoria and Karen made Mary promise she would call them if she needed them. They would also take her to the hospital when it was time and stay with her through the labor and delivery. Mary also knew her family would be there. That made her feel more secure. Most importantly, Jesus would be with her.

Mary would be off for a while, and she wanted to stock up on groceries and things she would need, so she wouldn't have to take the baby out, at least until her first follow-up appointment. She knew she would forget something, but she had been writing a list in her notes on her phone to try to get all she needed. She spent more than an hour in the store, gathering all the items on her list and picking up other things she had forgotten to add.

After arriving home, she put the groceries away and took JJ for a walk. She put her pajamas on and decided to relax for the rest of the evening.

She spent the next day doing laundry. She washed the baby's clothes and put them away in the baby's small dresser against the wall. She put all her gifts away, making sure they were all sanitized and clean.

Later in the day, she was sitting on her bed and writing in her journal when the pain hit her. She was startled and began to panic. "Oh no! Is it time?" She quickly called Victoria.

Victoria answered the call quickly. "Mary, are you OK?"

"Victoria, I think I am in labor!"

"I'll be there in just a few minutes, Mary. Continue to rest."

Victoria ran to her car and called Karen on the way. They both met Mary at the cottage and spent some time with her. Mary was having some pain, but the contractions were not coming often. Karen agreed to stay with her through the night. She would be there if Mary needed to go to the hospital and to let JJ out so Mary wouldn't have to go outside. Victoria stayed longer and made Karen and Mary promise to call if they went to the hospital. They promised they would.

They spent a few hours talking, and occasionally, Mary would have a contraction. She talked about Michael and wondered where he was and how he could walk away like that. Victoria didn't understand either. Mary had not heard a word from him since he'd left the cottage that day. Now, instead of a husband, Mary had to rely on her friends to help—mostly Jesus, though. She knew He was with her. First Corinthians 2:9 comforted her: "What no eye has seen, what no ear has heard, and what no human mind has conceived the things God has prepared for those who love him." God knew Mary loved Him. She wasn't perfect, and He knew that too.

At three o'clock in the morning, Mary's water broke. Karen was right there. Mary already had a bag packed in case they needed to leave quickly. Karen helped Mary get dressed, ran JJ out for a quick walk, put down his and Sunshine's food, and helped Mary to the car. "I think it's time for a sweet blessing, Mary," Karen said.

As they arrived at the hospital, Mary remembered to call her sister Sarah. Sarah would then call Beth and their dad. Sarah picked up the phone and Mary said, "I am at the hospital now. I promised I would let you know."

Sarah was excited and called the others. They planned to meet at Sarah's house in thirty minutes to get on the road. The drive went quickly, and they were all excited about the arrival of Mary's baby. They knew that as it was Mary's first baby, it might take a while.

Mary was admitted to the hospital and was resting. Karen was sitting by her when her family walked in. Her contractions were coming a lot quicker than they all had expected so early into labor. Before they all knew it, the nurses were clearing the room, and one said, "It's time to push,

Mary." Mary looked over to see her dad standing behind the curtain with Karen. Sarah stayed in the room to encourage Mary.

Soon after she began to push, Mary heard a cry. Her baby had been born into the world. Through her tears, she saw the nurses cleaning her up. Seconds later, she felt her baby lying on her chest. It was the most incredible feeling she had ever felt. As tears fell down her cheeks, she began to pray. "Thank you, Lord, for my sweet baby. She is a miracle from heaven. She is perfect, Lord. Help me, please, to teach her the way she should go and to be a great mom for her. In Jesus's name, amen."

Mary's dad and sisters found their way into the room even before everyone was cleaned up. They were happy for Mary. They loved Mary and wanted everything to be perfect in her life.

Mary had thought of many names but had not decided. However, as soon as she felt her daughter next to her, she knew it right away. Mary would name her after her grandmother Lizzie, who had been one of the strongest, godliest women in Mary's life. She would call her Elizabeth.

Elizabeth would change Mary's life forever, and never in her lifetime, other than the love of Jesus, had she understood the word *love* as she knew it now. Other than Jesus, Elizabeth was the most important person in her life. Mary would sacrifice all she had for her, and Elizabeth would always, after Jesus, be the first place in her heart.

Mary spent one night in the hospital, and Karen and Victoria took turns checking on JJ and Sunshine. Karen decided to spend the night at the cottage because she knew Mary would be resting. Karen's husband, Sam, loved her heart and wanted to be there for her friend, so he agreed that her staying over would be great. Karen also wanted Mary to have time privately in the room with Elizabeth.

Mary's dad and sisters had rooms at the inn. Mr. Henry made sure they were comfortable and had all they needed. He never let them pay for their rooms or the food while there, and it was always his pleasure to serve them. They loved the service the inn provided and never took it for granted. Mary was happy they had a place to stay that they loved.

The time came for Mary and Elizabeth to go home. They were both doing well. Mary was excited and nervous. Her dad and sisters picked her up at the hospital and had Elizabeth's new car seat strapped in. Mary chose to put a sweet outfit on her that her sister Sarah had given her. She was wrapped in the crocheted blanket Beth had made, warm socks, and a knit hat. She was the most beautiful baby Mary had ever seen. Mary knew she was perfect, exactly as Jesus had made her.

She remembered the words of Psalm 139:14: "I praise you because I am fearfully and wonderfully made; your works are wonderful; I know that full well."

After they arrived home, she sat down on the couch and called JJ over to meet Elizabeth. Sunshine was curious too. Her sisters made some lunch for all of them and helped Mary get comfortable. They brought the bassinet to the living room so they could all admire the baby for a while. Mary was overwhelmed with the blessing of Elizabeth in her life and knew the next few years would be challenging but rewarding.

Mary was tired, as she had been up most of the night. Elizabeth enjoyed sleeping through the day and wanted to be up most of the night. Mary knew she needed to try to get her on a better schedule, as she would go back to work in a few weeks. She wished she never had to leave her, but she knew she would not have that choice. Mary decided she would interview nannies over the next couple of weeks to find someone to stay with Elizabeth at home during the day. That would be hard for Mary; she prayed she would find the perfect one.

A couple of weeks passed, and Mary was adjusting well to having Elizabeth. She loved the time they had together and decided for the first time to take her out to the beach for a walk. She would try taking her in the stroller. The walk would be nice for both. She thought about taking JJ but thought she'd better wait until the next time. She had a baby-wrap carrier she could use when taking JJ for a walk so her hands would be free, but this time, they would go alone.

As Mary walked the beach, pushing the stroller, she thought of Elizabeth as a toddler and how much they would enjoy the ocean. Mary hoped the cottage would always be their home. Being a single mom had a lot of challenges, but she never thought of it that way. Mary only knew that Elizabeth was a gift, and she thanked God for her every day. She began her mornings by reading God's Word to Elizabeth and praying. Elizabeth seemed to enjoy Mary's reading to her.

Elizabeth was growing fast, and Mary knew time would pass quickly. Before she knew it, Elizabeth would be out of college, but she wasn't ready to think about those days.

Six weeks passed, and it was time for Mary to go back to work. She began to cry, thinking of leaving Elizabeth. She had been busy with her book, and time had gone by quickly. She thought another week off would be nice if it were possible. She decided to call Mr. Henry. If the intern could work another week, maybe she would have another week at home. She picked up the phone to call. When he answered, he knew what she was going to ask for before she asked and told her not to worry. He had already talked to the intern, who'd agreed to stay another week.

Mary was happy to have another week off with Elizabeth but knew she had to somehow prepare herself for going back to work next week. God spoke to Mary with the words in Isaiah 46:4: "Even to your old age and gray hairs I am he, I am he who will sustain you. I have made you, and I will carry you; I will sustain you, and I will rescue you."

Mary loved how God carried her through every day. He was her strength, and she knew it above all else.

The next week, Mary did all she could to prepare herself to go back to work. She had the nanny come over for three days to spend with Elizabeth, as she wanted to be sure the nanny knew her routine, and Mary had to know she trusted her. Mary could tell the nanny enjoyed taking care of Elizabeth and was also good with JJ as well as Sunshine. She felt good about her decision and a little more prepared to leave her daughter.

The time came, and Mary got dressed for work. Elizabeth's nanny was at the door. As Mary went to the door to let her in, the realization that she had to leave Elizabeth hit her. She let the nanny in and prayed, *Father, please protect Elizabeth today, as I must go back to work. Please allow them to bond, and may the nanny treat Elizabeth with the grace and love that comes from you. In Jesus's name, amen.*

***

It seemed like yesterday that Mary had left Elizabeth for the first time to go back to work, but a year had passed. Elizabeth was beginning to take a few steps, and Mary thanked God that she was home to see her first one. Her first birthday party was in a couple of days; more than thirty-five people had RSVP'd that they would be there. Mary had a great, supportive group of friends and family, and they were all excited about celebrating the big occasion. She had decided to have the party at the cottage. She knew the space would be limited but wanted to have it at home. The weather was supposed to be beautiful, and she prayed that didn't change.

As Mary prepared her list of items to pick up at the grocery store, Elizabeth sat on the floor and played with some toys. She was more beautiful than ever. Mary loved it when she would utter the word *Mama*. She could feel the peace of Elizabeth, and it reminded Mary of Isaiah 54:13: "And all thy children shall be taught of the Lord, and great shall be the peace of the children."

Mary talked about the Lord continuously to her daughter and prayed with her daily. Elizabeth would know her Father in a real way. Mary would be sure of that.

The day of Elizabeth's first birthday party had arrived. Mary had everything ready: party hats, balloons, streamers, cupcakes, fruit trays, vegetable trays, and a table for the gifts. Elizabeth wore a casual but cute navy-blue two-piece set with red in it, and she was adorable.

The guests started to arrive. Her dad, Sarah, and Beth were in town and staying at the inn. They had planned to be there early to help Mary with any last-minute things that needed to be done.

Patricia and Paul were already there with Faith, and Faith and Elizabeth were playing in her room. Elizabeth's crib would soon be a toddler's bed, and Mary couldn't believe how quickly time had passed.

When Karen arrived, Mary noticed she had a bottle of champagne but didn't say anything. She wondered why she would bring champagne to Elizabeth's first birthday party.

When all the guests had arrived, Mary's dad asked if he could lead them in prayer. They all gathered, and he began to pray. "Father, thank you for allowing us to be together today for such an awesome celebration of Elizabeth's first birthday party. This year has gone by so fast, and it seems like yesterday that they both came home from the hospital. Thank you for the strength you have given my daughter to get through this first year, and as

I watch her continue to grow, I thank you for my granddaughter, Elizabeth. Father, you have blessed our family so well, and we are overwhelmed with gratitude for your mercy and grace in our lives. We pray as this celebration begins that you bless the food and everyone here and may they all know how much you love them. In Jesus's name, amen."

He asked if anyone else had anything to say, and Karen spoke quickly. She ran into the cottage and brought back the bottle of champagne and cups. She poured everyone a small glass and asked if she could toast Mary for such a successful year. As everyone stood listening to Karen, she said, "Mary, we not only celebrate Elizabeth's birthday today, but we also celebrate you. We have watched you grow into a beautiful mom for Elizabeth, and the selfless acts you have shown us this year have been noticed. God not only gave you a beautiful gift in Elizabeth, but He also gave us all a beautiful gift in you. You have given your all to us, and we thank you! Cheers, Mary! You made it through the first year!"

Mary couldn't have asked for a better party for Elizabeth, and the gifts she received were all special. She and Faith played with each toy, it seemed, and the cottage was a mess. As she looked around at all of it, she just smiled and thanked Jesus for a beautiful day.

Everyone was beginning to leave, and Mary was exhausted. Elizabeth had become fussy, and she was well overdue for her nap. When everyone was gone, Mary decided she would lay Elizabeth down on her bed to sleep, and she would take a nap with her. JJ also came up and joined them.

Before she knew it, she woke up from her nap, and two hours had passed. She looked over at Elizabeth, who was still sleeping. She put her arm around her and thought about the last year, including all the late-night feedings and the exhaustion she'd felt at work. She thought of the beautiful memories of her growing up, and she couldn't imagine her life without her.

Mary thought about her nanny. Sometimes, she missed her, but Elizabeth was doing well in the day-care center she had found. It had great reviews, and everyone in town loved the owners. They were careful to pay close attention to each child and make sure the center was run professionally. Elizabeth loved it there, and Mary knew she was safe.

***

Months and years passed, and Elizabeth grew up to be the sweetest child. She had the most precious personality and was always respectful. On her first day of kindergarten, Mary drove to the school and parked instead of going through the carpool line. Elizabeth was wearing a light blue skirt, a cute matching top, and white tennis shoes. Mary had brushed her hair and put it in a ponytail. Elizabeth was ready for a big school. As she got out of the car, carrying her lunch box, Mary began to cry. She couldn't believe she had to leave her in this big place, and she was not going to let her walk in by herself.

Three weeks passed, and Mary was still walking Elizabeth into class when the principal stopped her in the hallway one day. "Mary, can I speak to you for a minute?"

After Mary walked over to see her, the principal told her she had to start letting Elizabeth out at the carpool line. Elizabeth gave her a look as if to say, "Mom, it's OK. I am a big girl now."

Mary looked at the principal and said, "I can't."

She responded, "You must. Tomorrow morning, please let her off at the carpool line."

Mary cried all the way to work, wondering how she would ever do this.

The next morning came, and Mary drove her to school. She didn't know how she would do what she needed to do, but she knew she had to. As they drove into the school parking lot, she got in the carpool line. As they reached the entrance to the school, Elizabeth kissed Mary on the cheek, opened the door, and said, "Love you, Mom."

Before Mary started to drive away, she was sobbing. She cried all the way to work and knew she would not get over this one anytime soon. She also knew she would never forget that moment. She thought it was a moment of letting go of her baby that she wasn't quite ready for. She began to pray. "Father, please protect my daughter. In Jesus's name, amen."

There had been many moments in life like that for Mary since Elizabeth was born. Mary was a protective mom. She knew how cruel the world could be and would do whatever she could to protect her from evil.

18

ANOTHER TEST OF FAITH

It was eight o'clock in the morning, and Mary was sitting at her desk at work. Months had passed, and she was busier than she had ever been. Elizabeth was starting her third year of elementary school, and Mary was continuing to try to maintain a balance in her life, but with her daughter, work, and another book being published, her time for anything else was limited. Elizabeth attended most of her book signings. They had become a team, and everyone loved her. Mary thought maybe she would be an author one day as well. God had used her books to encourage so many hearts, and she loved the ministry side of her writings. The conversations that Mary was blessed with were encouraging for her. It lightened the pain to know God was using it all for His glory.

As she walked into the restaurant to grab a cup of coffee, she ran into Mr. Henry. "Hi there, young man," she said. "You're looking great these days. How are you feeling?" He had aged quite a bit over the years, but Mary was happy God had healed him of his cancer. He was grateful, too, and was happy to be still working. Mary was happy she had followed her heart and had not taken his position. God had known all along that Mr. Henry would still be working.

After Mary got back to her desk, a tall, blond-haired guy walked in and introduced himself as Jimmy. She reached for his hand to shake it and said, "Hi, Jimmy. My name is Mary. I am the sales and marketing director here at the inn. Come in and have a seat."

He said he was from the Mercy Center, and they were helping a woman in need by having a preowned manufactured home set up for her. He was seeking a possible room donation for her as her home was being set up.

Mary began asking questions about the lady and why she needed the help. Jimmy told her that her name was Ms. Lizzy. She didn't have any family and was living in a home with holes in the floors. "Her place is in the woods, so we will have to do some tree work around there for the home mover to get in. It will probably be a minimum of two weeks before she will need the room."

Mary told him she would talk to the general manager about it and get back to him. She knew she could make the decision but wanted to at least mention it to him, and it would also give her some time to think about it.

As he got up to leave, God showed her a glimpse of Jimmy's heart. She thought he was a humble man—maybe a pastor. She didn't understand what was going on. *Is this who he is, Lord?* An experience like this had never happened to Mary before.

Mary heard God speak in a kind voice: "Mary, love him, and keep this relationship pure."

In her confusion, she stopped him before he left her office, and she asked if she could have a picture with him. She had no idea what that was about, and she didn't mention anything to him, as she needed to pray for clarity and try to understand what was going on. He left and said he would be back tomorrow around noon.

The entire rest of the day felt a little confusing, as Mary could not understand what God was asking of her about Jimmy, the guy who'd walked into her office that morning. She was confused and needed to understand. She began to pray. *Father, please protect me. Did you just tell me to love him and keep this relationship pure?*

Mary heard the words of Matthew 8:26: "And he saith unto them, why are ye fearful, O ye of little faith?" She knew what she had heard. She had prayed that if she were ever to be married again, God would send her a godly man, but who was this man? Where did he come from?

It was close to five, and she had to pick Elizabeth up at gymnastics camp. Mary didn't like having her go to camp after school each day, but she always found interesting activities and places where Elizabeth was well cared for while she was at work. Elizabeth also enjoyed it. Occasionally, Mary had to work late, but her friends were always willing to pick Elizabeth up, and with Karen being at home, she was available most of the time. Karen had not gotten pregnant yet but knew her time would come. Faith was always happy when Patricia could pick Elizabeth up, as they enjoyed spending time together.

Elizabeth decided she wanted pizza for dinner, so they stopped to pick up a pizza at their favorite Italian restaurant on their way home. Mary wanted spaghetti and thought she would get an order of it and would also have some left over for lunch the next day.

After dinner, they both showered and then snuggled while reading together. Elizabeth enjoyed listening to the email responses from Mary's readers about her books. She had developed into a little witness of Jesus, too. She had been with Mary at the inn one day, and when a contractor had come to repair an AC unit, Elizabeth had looked at him and said, "Did you know Jesus is in my heart?" That had happened a few times. Randomly, Elizabeth would share about Jesus. The contractor had been touched by her words.

They talked about Jesus a lot and prayed together every day. Mary loved every scripture in God's Word, but one of her favorites she prayed over Elizabeth continuously was Psalm 91:4: "He will cover you with his feathers, and under his wings, you will find refuge; his faithfulness will be your shield and rampart." Mary knew the Lord would always be with them.

Morning came, and Mary and Elizabeth dressed and had breakfast. As Mary left her bedroom, she walked by a picture she and Elizabeth had bought at an antique store on a rainy day a few years back. As she walked by, the Lord said, "Take that to Jimmy." She didn't hesitate; she took it off the nail on the wall, walked into the kitchen, and laid it by her purse so she would not forget it. The picture was in a simple frame and had two angels with the scripture 1 Corinthians 13:4–7: "Love is patient, love is kind. It does not envy, it does not boast, it is not proud. It does not dishonor others; it is not self-seeking. It is not easily angered; it keeps no record of wrongs. Love does not delight in evil but rejoices with the truth. It always protects, always trusts, always hopes, and always perseveres."

While driving Elizabeth to school, she thought about the picture and remembered the day they'd bought it. She'd had no idea why it was so special to her, but now she thought she knew. *Why does the Lord want me to give it to a stranger? And why are you calling me to love him, Lord?* In all her years of walking with Jesus, Mary had never been more puzzled at what God was doing.

After arriving at work, she saw Jimmy sitting in the lobby. As she walked in, he followed her to her office.

"Hi, Mary," he said. "I am so sorry to be bothering you so early this morning, but I wanted to get here early because we are trying to plan all the details for the delivery of Ms. Lizzy's home. Did you get an opportunity to talk to your boss?"

"Hi, Jimmy," Mary said. "I did, and we will be willing to offer a donation for a room for two weeks. Mr. Henry also said he would donate twenty dollars daily in meals for her."

Jimmy seemed pleased with the offer and thanked her. He asked her to thank Mr. Henry as well.

As he left, Mary said, "Oh, Jimmy, I am not sure why, but the Lord told me to give this to you." She handed him the picture.

He looked at her strangely and said, "OK, thank you, Mary."

Later that day, her cell phone rang, and it was Jimmy. He was inviting Mary to a hockey game that evening. She had no idea how she would go or who would watch Elizabeth, so she told him she would have to get back to him a little later. She quickly called her friend Karen to ask if she could watch Elizabeth at the cottage for a few hours. She told her about meeting Jimmy and how God had told her to love him. "Karen, this is weird, but I feel led to go. I need to get to know him and try to understand some of this."

Karen had no problem with watching Elizabeth. They could have a quick dinner and take JJ out on the beach for a while. They agreed to meet at the cottage at six. Mary would pick Elizabeth up at gymnastics camp.

Some of Jimmy's friends, a preacher, and his wife had invited him, and they would pick her up at six thirty. When Mary got home, she made a little dinner for the three of them and sat down to eat. Before she knew it, Jimmy and his friends were there. She introduced Karen to Jimmy and thanked her for watching Elizabeth.

The hockey game was fun, but what happened after was more than Mary thought she could handle. Jimmy told Mary that God had told him to be honest with her and tell her the truth about his life. He said it was the first time he had ever heard God speak. He told her he knew what it looked like, with his meeting her at the inn while seeking donations for Ms. Lizzy, but it wasn't what it looked like. He told her the Mercy Center was his call for help, and he knew the preacher and his wife because he had been there before. Mary looked at him strangely and wondered what in the world he was about to tell her.

Jimmy felt sure he would never see her again after this, but he told her he'd had a substance abuse issue and had lost his family, including his children.

Mary asked him to leave and said in a firm tone that wasn't what God had shown her. "I have to go pray." She was more confused now than ever and had no interest in following this plan. The Lord had given her a vision of something totally different about him. After all, she had prayed for a godly man if it was His will that she ever be married again. *His story doesn't sound like that of a godly man*, Mary thought.

Mary knew she must have been wrong in what she'd heard because she was aware of the scripture in 2 Corinthians 6:14: "Do not be yoked together with unbelievers: for what do righteousness and wickedness have in common? Or what fellowship can light have with darkness?"

She began to pray. "Father, I misunderstood you. There is no way you would have me love Jimmy with what seems like so much chaos in his life."

Mary heard God reply with Matthew 8:26: "You of little faith, why are you so afraid?"

The following day, before work, she went by the Mercy Center but never got out of the car. Jimmy was standing outside and saw her pull up. She rolled the window down and, in anger, said, "I hate drugs, I have never used drugs, drugs will never be part of my life, and God told me to love you." She then drove out of the parking lot.

Mary was as afraid as she had ever been. After all, she had a daughter she was protective of, and she knew this was nowhere close to a good fit for her, let alone Elizabeth.

Mary tried to embrace the test God had given her, but she wasn't handling it well. Jimmy called a couple of times and asked her for a date, and Mary was concerned. If she agreed to go out with Jimmy, she would only go on double dates with friends to avoid being alone with him.

What happened next changed Mary's perspective on everything. Standing at her kitchen sink one day, Mary questioned the Lord again. "Lord, this can't possibly be your plan for my life. Seriously?"

Something happened at that moment that was not easy for Mary to explain, but she knew exactly what she felt and heard that day. God surrounded her with His presence as if she weren't aware of her surroundings. He asked her, "Mary, do you remember the pain of childbirth? It's forgotten. Now is your time to mourn, but I will give you joy that no one can take away."

Just like that, Mary was back to the realization that she was standing at her sink, doing dishes. She then heard the Enemy say, "God didn't speak to you."

She argued with him, saying, "Yes, He did speak to me. I wouldn't have ever said this to myself. I didn't even know those words." Mary knew what God had said to her, but she continued to have questions.

God later confirmed through scripture, with John 16:21: "A woman giving birth to a child has pain because her time had come, but when her baby is born, she forgets the anguish because of her joy that a child is born into the world."

Everyone who knew Mary, including her family, questioned everything she was doing. They said, "You are so successful in business and intelligent. What are you doing with him?"

All Mary could say was, "I know this doesn't make sense. Trust me. It doesn't make sense to me, but God makes everything beautiful." Her faith was made real in Jesus.

While struggling to understand everything, Mary called their pastor to discuss her concerns. He asked her to give Jimmy the phone number of a gentleman he knew named Brian. Brian had a similar past, and the pastor suggested Jimmy visit Brian, as he felt Jimmy would enjoy hearing him share his testimony. He thought he could encourage him, and they could relate well to each other. Mary gave Jimmy the number, but with numerous excuses, he refused to go. Finally, Mary convinced him to go, and what happened next changed Jimmy's life forever.

Jimmy called Mary after he left Brian's house and sounded shaken up. He told her how Brian had left his career to do ministry full-time. Jimmy could not understand their conversation and said, "Who leaves a quarter-of-a-million-dollar-a-year job to serve Jesus?" Brian had asked to pray with him before he left. He had taken Jimmy's hands and begun to pray when Jimmy had felt a gust of wind go through his body. He said, "It felt like someone connected a jet dryer to the bottom of my feet, and it went through my body." He didn't know how long it had lasted or where it had come from. Jimmy later understood more of what Jesus was doing. John 3:8 says, "The wind blows wherever it pleases. You hear its sound, but you cannot tell where it comes from or where it is going. So it is with everyone born of the Spirit."

Jimmy was scared. He didn't know what had just happened to him. He told Mary that his hands were shaking so badly he couldn't get the keys in his truck's ignition.

Mary, crying, raised her hands to heaven and said, "Finally! The Lord has finally got you!"

Jimmy said, "Mary, I know Jesus Christ, and I know He died on the cross for my sins, but I can't believe He would ever touch me."

Jimmy didn't feel worthy of Jesus's love. He had run from God his entire life, as he had deep pain and dealt with it the only way he knew how. The sin was an escape from the reality of his life that he couldn't deal with. That saddened Mary, and she was finally beginning to understand some of what God was doing.

Three days later, Jimmy called to say he was going to cut some branches from a friend's tree close to her cottage. He needed to carve some shepherd staffs. He came over, sat on the deck of Mary's cottage, and shaved staffs until his hands were blistered and bleeding. Mary, filled with the Holy Spirit, cried and thanked Jesus for changing Jimmy's heart. In Corinthians 1:27–29, the Bible says, "But God chose the foolish things of the world to shame the wise; God chose the weak things of the world to shame the strong. God chose the lowly things of the world and the despised things—and the things that are not—to nullify the things that are so that no one may boast before him."

Jimmy called his friend the next day to tell him what had happened, and his friend was overjoyed but didn't understand the significance of the staff. Micah 7:14 says, "Shepherd your people with your staff, the flock of your inheritance, which lives by itself in a forest, in fertile pasturelands."

While Mary was sleeping one night, God woke her up at two o'clock in the morning to give her words of comfort from Ephesians 4:12–13: "To equip his people for works of service, so that the body of Christ may be built up until we reach unity in the faith and in the knowledge of the Son of God and become mature, attaining to the whole measure of the fullness of Christ." That was when the true reality set in. As Mary sat there in awe of what she had heard, she was overwhelmed by the grace of Jesus and said aloud, "This is what you're doing, Lord!"

Jimmy began praying with Mary and Elizabeth every day. Micah 6:8 says, "He has shown you, O mortal, what is good. And what does the Lord require of you? To act justly and to love mercy and to walk humbly with your God."

Mary's faith continued to grow, and as trials and doubt came in, God quickly reminded Mary of the words, "Oh ye of little faith. Where is your faith?"

Jimmy asked Mary to marry him several months later, and she said yes, realizing that now that they were equally yoked, God must have had grand plans for them as a couple and a family. After all, Jimmy had two additional children of his own. They would become a blended family. She realized that all things were possible with God, and living her life according to His plans was her first choice. She knew He would never leave or forsake her, and not only did Jimmy have much to learn, but Mary did, too.

Mary had not realized that God was changing her heart as much as He was changing Jimmy's. Mary had spent her entire life in the church and had not realized how judgmental she had been. God had put the love in her heart to love Jimmy. There was no other explanation. She was reminded of

2 Corinthians 5:17: "Therefore if anyone is in Christ, the new creation has come. The old is gone; the new is here."

The most significant part of the story is next, and there are many incredible blessings to follow. Mary's walk in faith, trust in Jesus Christ, and refusal to allow outside voices to change her decision were challenging, but the most outstanding picture of God's love and goodness was unfolding right before her eyes. Jeremiah 29:11 became one of their favorite scriptures: "For I know the plans I have for you declares the Lord, plans to prosper you and not to harm you, plans to give you hope and a future."

Mary knew she could not trust Jimmy, but she could trust Jesus, and He promised her in John 11:40, "Did I not tell you that if you believe, you will see the Glory of God?"

AFTERWORD

All scriptures used in this story are to remind us of how amazing God's love is. He loves us and can use our failures for our good. When we repent of our sins and trust Him, we can believe we will see the glory of God in our lives. Faith is believing in what we can't see.

Jesus loves us deeply, died a brutal death, and rose again on the third day for the sins of the entire world. Repent, ask Him for forgiveness, and ask Him to come into your heart today. He's waiting for you right now. He loves you deeply! God bless you, and my prayer is for everyone reading this story to come to know Jesus in a personal way. It will be the most critical decision you will ever make in your lifetime. Do not believe the lie. You are worthy! In Jesus's name.

Thank you for allowing me to share my heart with you and for your prayers and love. Please look for my next book as this story continues.

"May the God of hope fill you with all joy and peace as you trust in Him, so that you may overflow with hope by the power of the Holy Spirit." Romans 15:13

Blessings to you! Always Believe,
Martha Gayle

NEW INTERNATIONAL BIBLE SCRIPTURES FOR REFERENCE

Matthew 6:19–21

Revelations 2:4

Proverbs 4:23

Luke 23:34

Romans 8:28

John 19:30

Ephesians 4:32

Ecclesiastes 4:12

Matthew 6:14–15

Isaiah 53:5

Galatians 6:2

2 Timothy 3:16–17

Psalm 119:105

Galatians 6:2–5

Mark 5:19

John 15:13

Luke 12:12

1 Corinthians 6:18–20

Proverbs 4:23

Romans 8:28

Psalm 1:1–2

Proverbs 21:31

Isaiah 41:10

Proverbs 3:15

Jeremiah 29:11

Matthew 16:24

Galatians 2:20

Matthew 19:5

John 21:17

John 15:5

1 John 1:9	Matthew 8:26
Romans 8:28	1 Corinthians 13:4–7
2 Peter 3:8	John 16:21
Ecclesiastes 3:11	John 3:8
Psalm 139:13–14	Corinthians 1:27–29
Philippians 4:13	Micah 7:14
Psalm 91	Ephesians 4:12–13
1 Corinthians 2:9	Micah 6:8
Psalm 139:14	2 Corinthians 5:17
Isaiah 54:13	Jeremiah 29:11
2 Corinthians 6:14	John 11:40

Have there been any scriptures in God's Word through Mary's story that have changed your heart? Please respond to www.marthagayle.com and share your testimony there. I would love to hear from you.

Blessings,
Martha Gayle

STUDY NOTES

Made in United States
North Haven, CT
06 February 2024